BLOOD

JOHN BRUNI

Copyright © John Bruni
Cover by Matt Andrew
Edited by Nicholas Day
Published by Strangehouse Books
(an imprint of Rooster Republic Press)

www.roosterrepublicpress.com

Printed in the USA.

To everyone I've ever hurt, especially *you*. You'll know who you are after reading the prologue.

ACKNOWLEDGEMENTS

Once upon a time, I was getting absolutely trashed at the Spring Inn, which is a good place to talk to strangers. I have no idea what his name was, but he told me about his very specific method of coping with his rage. He told me that he carried an axe with him wherever he went, and if he was feeling angry, he would park his car and chop down the nearest tree. I don't know if you were full of shit or not, but thank you for sharing.

JOHN BRUNI
BLOOD

PROLOGUE

Mickey's knuckles groaned as he tightened his grip on his brother's throat. Rex's delicate blue eyes rolled back in his head, and his tongue peeked out from between his purple lips. One last whimper of air escaped from Rex's larynx before it closed entirely. Mickey's teeth ground like the back of a dump truck, but he didn't care.

Something roared in the background, but Mickey couldn't hear it clearly. He was in the zone, and he refused to leave it until—

"Goddammit! Let him go, you son of a bitch!"

Arms wrapped around Mickey's shuddering, taut form, and he barely noticed as thick, knotted fingers slithered around his hands, yanking the thumbs back. Pain jolted him, and Rex slipped from his grasp. Mickey bared his teeth, growling as he turned on whoever had saved his brother's life.

He saw his father. Maxwell Scarlet. All six-four of him, crouching like an animal ready to pounce. Mickey made no distinction between his old man and any other asshole. He sprang forward, one hand drawn back in a fist and the other extended like a claw.

Maxwell slammed his sharp knuckles into Mickey's cheek.

Lights out.

Fade in. Mickey fought through the mists until he could open his eyes and see clearly. His skull throbbed like it usually did when he got a wallop from his father. He tried to remember what had caused it this time, but nothing came to mind.

He saw he was on the couch, and he slowly sat up, mindful of the little men pounding away at the inside of his skull with pickaxes. His vision doubled up, but he shook his head, straightening everything out.

"You're awake."

Mickey squinted against the pain, shifting his gaze to the direction of the voice. Maxwell Scarlet sat in his usual chair, lounging back and drinking whiskey from a tumbler. A cigarette smoldered in a dingy ashtray with the faded image of an American flag in the bowl.

Maxwell didn't even look at his son. He kept his eyes focused on a TV that played only the color bars of a station no longer on the air. A dull tone hummed, filling the silence.

"Why?" Mickey asked.

"I was about to ask *you* that." Only now did the father take in the son. "Why did you try to kill Rex?"

"I . . ." It sounded vaguely familiar. The ghost

of his hands around his brother's throat. Nothing more. "I don't know."

Maxwell took a long drag off his cigarette and blew the smoke to the ceiling in a steady stream of dragon's breath. "Rex has a smart mouth on him. He say something? That it?"

"Maybe. I don't know. I don't remember."

Silently Maxwell stubbed out his cigarette. He stood and walked around the coffee table until he was in front of his son. There he sat and looked directly into Mickey's face. They each independently thought that they were looking into their own eyes, but they said nothing.

"You're my kid, all right. We got the same thing. I don't know if it's hereditary or if it's something I beat into you. I don't care. But if you let this thing take you over like you did today, you're not going to make it in his shit stain of a world."

Mickey broke his father's gaze. "I wanted Rex dead."

"I know. You're going to feel that same urge for the rest of your life. You need to control it, or it's going to put you in a cage like a goddam animal or worse."

Mickey glanced back up at Maxwell. "I need to let it out. If I don't, I'll explode. I feel it clawing inside of me all the time."

His father nodded. "I can't always control it myself. I guess that's why I'm so hard on you and your brother. And your mother." He leaned back and sighed. Intensity slowly drained from his bunched form.

"What can I do?" Mickey asked.

Maxwell thought about it for a moment, a

callused thumb rubbing at the deep cleft in his chin. He stood and went to the closet. When he came back, he held something. He pressed the long handle into his son's hands.

And he said one word: "Trees."

*

When Mickey Scarlet looked up into the rearview mirror, his brow shot a droplet of sweat into his right eye, setting his cornea on fire. Gritting his teeth, he jammed the back of his hand across the pain and scrubbed at it with his coarse arm hair. The car drifted, but he didn't notice until his hubcaps ground and sparked against the median.

"Shit!" He whipped the wheel around and set himself back on course. This time he grabbed a handful of shirt and ducked down to the right, making sure to keep his other eye on the road. Satisfied, he turned his gaze back to the mirror, surveying the never-ending strip of blacktop unwinding behind him. The city skyscrapers loomed in the distance, the tops of the tallest gleaming like gold as the sun started its descent. It comforted him to know the city was far behind him, along with the feds and that goddam Karnaki.

Or was that cocksucker at his house already?

Mickey liked living in the boonies far away from his work, far away from all the things that he'd witnessed, the things he'd caused. All the things that could ruin a family. Home was a refuge from the city, and the very idea of Karnaki rummaging through it left a sour taste in the back of his throat.

Mickey's giant thumb worked away at the cleft in his chin. His other hand creaked on the wheel. He looked into the mirror again. Nothing.

Sweat trickled down from his hairline again, and he could feel it pooling in his eyebrows.

Did Melissa know yet? He fucking hoped not. He'd have to burn that bridge when he crossed it.

A high-pitched jagged whine filled his ears, and he gagged when he realized that it was the nervous sound of his own laughter. Why was he laughing? What was happening to him?

"Christ," he muttered. His hand slapped at his forehead, and he attempted to dry his wet palm on the damp spot on his jeans. Sweat clung to him like slime.

Mickey's knuckles itched. They wanted to be fired into Karnaki's fat jiggling face. He wasn't entirely sure, but he thought the fed wore a toupee. Mickey wanted to knock it off Karnaki's greasy pate hard enough to make it fly like a crow.

A car flashed in the rearview mirror. He glanced up and gauged it at maybe a quarter of a mile behind him. Could it be a cruiser? The headlights looked like the kind on some of the state vehicles, and it sailed at a respectable distance back. A tail? Did he see a bar of flashers on its roof? Or was it maybe a rack? He thought about slowing down just so he could get a good look, to set his paranoia at ease, but he couldn't risk it. The sharks couldn't be too far behind.

Instead he stomped on the accelerator and thumbed more sweat from his brow. His hair hung down in strings around his eyes, and he ran his hand through it to slick it back and out of his line of vision. His heart roared from within, and he wondered what would happen if it gave out now. Wouldn't that be a kick in the ass?

The mirror. The car drew closer. No cop, at least not marked. Probably not undercover. Forget it.

He turned his attention back to the road and watched as the ribbon of pavement slipped under his hood as if eaten by the grill of his car. Not fast enough. He pounded the steering wheel with his hand and let out an inarticulate, primal howl. How could he have let things get so far?

He trembled, and rivulets of sweat ran down his entire body. A crunching sound filled his head, and he couldn't stop himself from grinding his teeth. How could he face Melissa like this?

He had to calm down. The radio. Right. His pale fingers shook like maracas as he hit the button on the dash, and an old rock tune filled the car. No, that reminded him too much of his father. He needed something smooth to soothe the beast clawing at the inside of his body. He hit the scanner but came up with nothing.

"Fuck!" he screamed. "Fuck! Fuck!" He brought the edge of his fist down on the radio, and something snapped behind the LED screen. No more sound except for the pounding of his own pulse.

But the beast remained, and it jabbered relentlessly in his mind.

He couldn't put it off any longer. He couldn't think of outrunning Karnaki and his feds. He *had to* take care of this immediately.

Without thinking, his hands twisted the wheel

until he could hear his tires squealing on gravel.

He leaped out of his car as if he were on a spring, and the air took some of the sweat away almost on contact. He went to the trunk and pulled out his old companion. The blade shone sharply after all of these years, ever since his father had given it to him. Mickey had kept it clean and free from rust. Only the handle had lost its lacquer, and a few splinters stuck out like porcupine quills. They felt right against his callused hands as he strode out to the side of the road. He jumped over the shallow ditch without even looking at it, and he surveyed the trees he saw. Most weren't worth it. They were skimpy, almost sickly, probably from all the fumes from cars passing by.

But then he saw the one he wanted. The trunk probably measured a couple of feet in diameter, and it looked healthy and young and strong. The canopy above was going to someday be thick and lustrous, and he could hear birds singing above his head.

Not for much longer. He didn't break his stride as he hefted the axe onto his shoulder, and he drove the blade against the bark as hard as he could. It bit deep, but the damage wasn't enough. Sap and splinters showered all around him as he hacked away at the trunk, roaring all the emotion out of him.

He didn't see a tree. He saw Karnaki's jolly-Saint-Nick face. He saw Sgt. Parker's gaunt frame. He saw all the bastards who wanted to put him away for life.

Mickey lost track of himself, and he didn't come back until the thump of the tree against the ground vibrated through his guts like bass in a nightclub. He panted, but the shakes were gone. The sweat had dried. The beast was at peace.

Empty, he walked back to his car and dumped the axe in the trunk. He resumed the drive home, never once looking into the mirror. The world passed by his windows almost passively as if he'd just smoked a pipe full of opium after downing several shots of absinthe.

He rolled down the highway and turned at the gravel road that ran up to his house. It was on about ten acres of land, and he kept meaning to find out how to farm it. The Job always occupied the important parts of his brain, and he never got around to it. Maybe when he was drawing his pension. Not now. Now he'd be lucky if the feds didn't seize all of his property.

Somehow as he pulled into his driveway and parked in front of his garage door, he thought he'd never see this place again.

No feds. No Karnaki. Good. They could have been hiding, but if so, they would have jumped on him.

Mickey eased out of his car, but he didn't make it far before the front door burst open. Melissa came waddling toward him, hands on both sides of her belly, which bulged out in front of her like a bowling ball. She moved barely faster than a stagger, and even at this distance, Mickey could see the shock on her face.

"Mickey! I saw you on TV!"

He wanted to hold her in his arms, and he rushed ahead to make it happen. But when he approached her, she stopped as if a defensive shield had gone up around her. He paused, searching her face.

"Is it true?" she asked.

He'd never wanted to lie to her over the course of their relationship. He'd always wanted to keep to the straight and narrow. This was possibly the most important moment they would share together short of the birth of their child. But he knew he couldn't let the truth out. Not now, not ever.

"Come on, honey. You know what the reporters are like."

"Don't give me that shit, Mickey. Just give me a yes or no answer. Did you do all of those things or not?"

Fuck. Shock was turning quickly into anger. He couldn't let that happen. He had to get the both of them away from here before Karnaki arrived. He let out a pained sigh. "Some of it. Not all of it. But some."

Her face tightened, and he could see her eyes moisten. "Did you kill that officer?"

"Goddammit, Melissa! I'm not a fucking animal!" It came out too loud, too angry, and he hated himself for it. He tried to search for a way to take back his tone, but the scared look on her face told him that he couldn't.

The tear spilled over Melissa's lower eyelid and cut across her cheek. "I don't know if I can trust you anymore." Her words crawled over his ears like crippled bugs. "I know what you're like sometimes." And now the tears blazed out of her down to the ledge of her jaw. But she didn't sob. She never closed her eyes against her husband.

Sirens in the distance. Mickey didn't need to glance back to know that Karnaki would be here very soon. He held Melissa's gaze. He wanted to hold her arms up high in a reassuring fashion, but he didn't think she would allow him to do that.

"Whatever I've done, and I've done a few things—shit, you can't stay away from it on the Job—you've got to know that I'd never hurt you or our baby. Shit, honey. I love you. If I didn't have you, I don't know what I'd do."

She sniffled, and the breeze blew back her hair. A single strand stuck to her wet cheek, and he wanted to push it away and behind her ear.

"Please. I love you."

She nodded, but she didn't look very convinced. "What are you going to do?"

"We're getting out of here," Mickey said. "Grab everything that's valuable. We gotta get going and fast." He put a hand on her shoulder to turn her back toward the house, but she shrugged away from him.

"I can't go with you. Our baby . . ."

"Jesus Christ, you have to!" Mickey recognized the panic in his voice and tried to dial it back down. "You have to. If these guys catch me, I'm going to prison for a long time. Forever. I'm not going to survive that. You know how they treat cops in there."

"Go without us," she said. "You'd probably have a better chance without us holding you up."

"What?! That's bullshit! Without you, none of this is worth it! Why do you think I did all of this stuff? It was so our kid could grow up in luxury!"

She gagged. "Don't say things like that."

Mickey drew his breath to yell again, but he could see he was losing her. He had to try something else. He forced himself to calm down. "It's true, though. You know how I grew up. I don't want that for our kid."

"Mickey! We can't raise a child like that! Not with . . . with dirty money!"

"Why not? I keep you guys away from everything I do. You're all clean. The money is pretty clean."

She retreated a few steps, cradling her belly. "Please. Just go. Don't bring us into it."

Mickey finally turned around, and he could see police cars in the distance. Some were state. Others were city, probably just there to watch the show or offer moral support. The vehicles that scared him were the ones that were completely black with the large antennas on the backs.

He bit his lips. "Come on, Mel. Please. Don't do this to me. I need you. I love you. If you don't come with me, this is all for nothing."

She couldn't control it any longer; her body shook with the force of her sobs. Her eyes lwere dark, with thinly-lined bags hanging under them. "You have no idea how much you scare me sometimes."

"Scare you?!" he yelled. His fists bunched up at his sides, and he could feel all control slipping away. "How the fuck do I scare you?! What's so fucking scary about me?!"

She hunched down and couldn't look him in the eyes. "You're scaring me right now." Her voice sounded thin, like a little girl's. "You've always had this violent streak in you, and now I'm afraid that you've actually killed someone. I can't go on the road with you. We can't raise our baby on the run. Not with someone who has a . . . a . . . beast living inside of him."

The world around Mickey shrank away. All he could see was his wife's cowering form, and sheer rage boiled within him. "So . . . what?! This is it?! You're fucking leaving me *now*?!"

She cringed, squinting her eyes shut. "I left you a long time ago. You've just been too involved in your double-dealing to notice."

His thick hands throbbed, and the beast crawled out of his belly again. "Are you . . . are you saying what I think you're saying?"

She didn't speak a word.

"Holy fuck. Is this kid even mine?"

Silence.

The sound of wood splintering echoed in Mickey's mind. His hands itched to hold the axe again, but he wasn't sure if it was a tree he wanted to cut down this time.

The vehicles came up the gravel drive, and in seconds they would be in firing range. He felt in his guts that Karnaki rode in the front car. He could almost see the fat cocksucker behind the wheel with his stupid mirrored glasses and the ugly ragged cigar in his mouth.

No escape. And he couldn't give the bastard the satisfaction of taking him down. Mickey stormed past Melissa as if she wasn't there anymore. She cringed and leaped back, nearly tumbling over her own feet. She managed to regain her balance, gripping her belly with both hands, but Mickey didn't even glance at her. He opened the front door so swiftly he flung it off its hinges, and he pounded up the stairs so loudly he cracked the wood beneath his feet.

In their bedroom—no, *his* bedroom now—he went to the closet and took down the gun safe. This he kept for protection, and it was not registered anywhere, just in case he needed a cold piece. Today he needed it for something else. He whipped through the combo and checked to make sure the gun was loaded.

Outside his window he could see the police cars coming to a stop. Gravel kicked up dust clouds thick enough to almost obscure the image of Melissa hugging herself, watching as Karnaki and the bastards emerged from their vehicles.

Mickey stuck the barrel into his mouth, pressing it against his palate. He'd seen enough failed suicides to know that he wanted to do this right. He gagged against the cold metal and the oil, and he knew this would be right. In moments he wouldn't be human anymore. He'd look more like a Hollywood prop than anything that once lived.

He tightened his grip, and something clicked and drew back inside the gun. Tension increased on his creaking finger, and he could feel the world shifting around him. Something different buzzed through reality, and existence seemed to be fundamentally changed. He couldn't tell what it was, but he knew nothing would ever be the same again.

Someone called out his name through a bullhorn. Karnaki. Even his voice sounded fat. There were more words, pleas, but he didn't pay attention. None of that mattered anymore. The corners of his eyes dripped, and he wanted nothing more than to have it all go away.

"Fuck that shit, son."

Mickey glanced to the closet, and from between his shirts and suits, a thick, gnarled hand oozed, parting his clothes to reveal a block of a man. Maxwell Scarlet. A third eye, this one red and swimming with blood, leered at Mickey from the center of the old man's forehead. Gore dribbled down Maxwell's face in an unending river of crimson.

"You don't want to off yourself." When Maxwell spoke, his lips did not move. A calm, eerie grin stood cemented in place, showing off tombstone teeth from a forgotten cemetery. A cold, cheerless gleam came from his other eyes, the ones he'd been born with. "Take that fucking gun from your mouth, you crybaby."

Mickey's finger relaxed, but he didn't move the metal from the roof of his mouth.

"The beast," Maxwell said. "You've always wanted an excuse to let it out. Let it take over. Let it live your life. Now is the time. You're going to prison for the rest of your life. What reason do you have to put on a show of playing by the rules?"

No. Maxwell couldn't be right. The beast wasn't something to be proud of, something to give full reign to. The beast was a curse, and it could never be let loose.

"Who gives a fuck if you beat the living daylights out of a bunch of criminals? You can bite out throats, Mickey. You can tear off faces. You can literally rip men apart with your bare hands. These are all things you've wanted to do ever since you were a boy. Now you can do them."

Mickey thought back to the first time he'd ever held an axe and used it against a tree. He remembered watching the utter destruction of a thing that would have gone on living hundreds of years without his intervention. Something that would make a difference in the world. Taking that away made him feel all powerful. It made him feel like he had a place in the world. It filled him with a sense that he was a force of nature, not just a mere man.

"The beast isn't a curse," Maxwell said. "It's a gift."

Gently he wrapped his monstrous hands around Mickey's gun hand and drew it back out of Mickey's mouth. A gooey strand of saliva connected his lips to the steel barrel, and it snapped, reeling back into place, leaving a wet trail from Mickey's mouth to his chin.

Maxwell took the gun to the closet and put it back in the safe. He turned and drew back to where he'd come from, fading like a shadow.

Mickey stared after him, wondering if his father —who had been dead for so many years—really was there. "Am I really that crazy?" he muttered.

All that remained of Maxwell's head was the grin, like the Cheshire cat. "Of course you are. Trust me, I should know. I made you."

And the grin disappeared.

Mickey blinked and looked at his empty hands. Sweat sheened over his palms, and his fingers trembled like a drunk's. Tiny crescents from his fingernails shone back up at him, pale and already fading.

He laughed. Of course. It made sense. It all made sense.

Mickey Scarlet stood and ambled down the stairs. Once outside the door, he raised his hands and placed them firmly on the top of his head. The cops swarmed him, and Karnaki watched smugly as they brought Mickey down and cuffed him and dragged him to the back of a cruiser.

They hadn't done so politely. One of his eyes puffed out, and a split brow dribbled blood in a steady stream. None of the authorities could explain the distant grin on his face, though, not even Melissa, who watched the whole thing as if they'd been clubbing her own child and dragging him away. She pinched her eyes shut, and that was fine with Mickey. He didn't want to look at her, either.

CHAPTER ONE

The cracked mirror over the dirty basin betrays very little of his age, but Mickey Scarlet can barely believe he's forty-five years old today. He keeps his hair crew-cut short—so no one can easily grab it—and it has not receded in the slightest. A bit of grizzle lit up the area above his ears ever so slightly, but only if seen from one angle and in the right light. Very few wrinkles crease his face, and his teeth are strong and in great condition.

But his eyes can't hide anything. Looking into his own emerald greens—just like his old man's —he thinks he might be seventy years old.

Something rattles behind him, and he whirls, fists clenched, adrenaline turning every nerve in his body on full-force. He thrums, ready.

It's only Sean, one of the guards. He moves his baton along the bars of the cell, but as soon as he sees Mickey's face, he jerks back as if he's touched a live wire.

Mickey forces his hands to uncoil. "What's up, Sean?"

The guard blinks, but his eyes quickly resume their usual size, and his tremulous hands put his baton back on his belt. "Warden wants to see you."

Mickey nods and holds out his wrists, ready for the customary handcuffs.

"No need," Sean says. "Come on."

For the first time since Mickey was locked away in this place, he feels nervous. This break in protocol is unheard of, and from all of his experience, this means there is a set-up in the works. He tries to think back on what he might have done to piss the guards off. He hasn't kicked the shit out of anyone in about a year. Who paid them to do this?

He steps back. "I'd rather not."

"It's not like that," Sean says. "It's gonna be fine."

Mickey does not want to be led into the warden's office, unrestrained, only to be shot in the head trying to "escape." His reputation is too strong. No jury would think twice.

"Cuff me," he says.

Sean laughs, but Mickey can see the sweat trickling and pooling in the V of his throat. "You're crazy, Mickey."

"Do it."

Sean shrugs and steps forward, encircling Mickey's wrists with cold steel between the bars. Mickey feels the clasps tug at his arm hair before they lock into place. He tightens each ring as much as he can until the metal bites into his flesh.

"What are you doing?" Sean asks.

"Making sure. If you guys kill me, there will at

least be ligature marks proving I was cuffed."

Sean laughs again, but his lips make no shape that could even loosely be identified as a smile. "Come on, Mickey. You're luckier than you can ever know."

The guard's words send a chill through Mickey's neck, but he doesn't know why. He watches the guard open the cell, and he lets himself be led down the corridor through a series of cages and locked doors. If anyone else had made such a walk, the other prisoners would have hooted and hollered and made kissy sounds. No one does this to Mickey. They know better.

The warden's office is cool and sparse. It lacks the warmth of a regular work place. Most desk-bound souls kept pictures of their families next to their calendars, but Samuel Kratz keeps nothing. He doesn't even wear his wedding ring, although its existence is proven by the pale sliver around his finger.

The walls bear no paintings; instead there are countless certificates and lithographs of the Constitution and other various law documents. Only a picture of the president of the United States seems to have a place of honor by the mounted flags behind the desk.

Sean leads Mickey through the room and stands him before the warden's desk. Kratz is a bent-over middle-aged man with silver, thinning hair and liver spots all over the backs of his arthritic hands. His bulb of a nose holds up his skinny spectacles, through which peers a set of beady blue eyes.

"I thought I said no handcuffs."

"Prisoner insisted," Sean says.

"Remove them at once."

"I'd prefer to keep them on," Mickey says. "At least until I'm back in my cell, if that's all right with you."

Kratz chuckles. "As you wish. Have a seat."

Mickey deems this safe enough, so he eases his considerable frame into the chair opposite of the desk, keeping his hands in plain sight the whole time. There is no cushion, and the seat feels like stone.

Kratz dismisses Sean with a wave of his hand and turns his full attention to the prisoner before him. "Paranoid, Mr. Scarlet?"

"Call it instinct. It's the only thing that's kept me alive this long."

"So I've noticed." Kratz opens the folder in front of him and leafs through a few pages, but he doesn't look at them. "Your file is a hell of a read. Did you really kill Sgt. Parker?"

"What do you think?"

Kratz's eyes turn to steel. "I think you're guilty as sin. But what I think doesn't matter much."

He clears his throat and closes the folder. He holds it in a hand shaped like a pallid tree root. He trembles but not with fear. A fire burns too brightly in the windows to his soul.

Kratz throws the file into the trashcan. "I've been in this business a long time. Longer than you've been alive, I'll wager. Before this, I was a low-level politician. I've seen my share of corruption. Hell, I've taken part in my share of dirty deals. Does my candor surprise you?"

Mickey keeps quiet.

"You clearly know a lot of people in high places, Mr. Scarlet. I think these are the guys who helped scrap that murder one charge, but what do I care?"

A lot, Mickey thinks. An apathetic person very rarely shakes with rage.

"If it was anyone else in this hellhole, I would

have said no. I would have given them their money back and sent them on their way. But you're a model prisoner, at least on paper. I'm pretty sure it was you who cut Jake Peterson's face off with a toothbrush shank, and if you didn't break Delroy Washington's neck, I'll cut off my own pecker and eat it with ranch dressing. But we never had anything on you. You're always so very-fucking-careful."

Again, Mickey keeps quiet. His face remains a still pond, serene and calm.

"I'm going to be blunt with you, Mr. Scarlet. I think you make my prison ten times more dangerous than it would have been before. Violence grows on you like grass on shit, and there's nothing that will ever change that. I'll go you one further: I think you inflict such violence because you can get away with it in here. Chances are, you're right. Outside, I don't think you could keep it up. Sure, you'll beat the shit out of someone every once in a while to stay in practice, but I don't think your wholesale brand of violence would continue so prolifically."

Mickey doesn't give an inch. Curiosity rises, but he keeps it in check.

"I've been paid a million dollars to let you go free," Kratz says. "One million dollars. It's hidden in various places all over my home right now."

"You're joking," Mickey says. "Who would pay a million bucks to spring me? In seven or eight years, I'll be out on parole."

"You'd be denied," Kratz says. "Believe me, I know the board. They like to stick it to corrupt cops. You'd have done your full stretch."

"It doesn't matter. I don't know anyone who would put up that much for my freedom. It just doesn't make sense."

"They know you. I wish I could tell you who it was. *I* don't even know. But the cash is real. Tomorrow morning, you'll be a free man, and all records of your existence here will be expunged."

Max leans back in his chair and tries to breathe, but his lungs are locked. Freedom! All he has to do is last until morning, and he'll no longer be a prisoner. But what about the people who arranged this? A million dollars to get him out of prison?

Never mind that. I'll finally be able to meet my kid.

While he'd been on trial, he'd demanded a paternity test, and after a lot of back and forth, Melissa granted it to him. The kid was his, all right, but Melissa made it damned near impossible to find out more information. After all of these years, Mickey still doesn't know if he has a son or daughter. He doesn't have a name. He doesn't have a picture. Nothing.

"I have a guy doctoring your records," Kratz says. "As far as the public is going to know, you're dead. Died before you even got to this prison. Is that understood?"

Mickey nods.

Kratz yanks his glasses off and buries his face in his palms. "Christ, why do I get the feeling that this is a huge mistake?"

"Probably because it's so illegal," Mickey says.

Kratz looks up and laughs. "Maybe." He spears his glasses back in place. "Look. I don't know who these people are, but they clearly want something from you. Something big. I suggest you don't do it. Make it a little easier on my ulcer, okay?"

Mickey shrugs. "If they have that much money, they'll probably get me to do anything."

Kratz nods. "Of course."

CHAPTER TWO

When Mickey Scarlet steps into the outside world for the first time in seven years, he doesn't have much to his name. The clothes on his back, a couple of pens, a notebook, a wallet containing an expired drivers license and a bunch of outdated credit cards and a couple of pictures of Melissa. He also has a check for two thousand dollars and a bus ticket. Everything he earned in all his time behind bars.

As he approaches the bus stop he sees an old man leaning against the sign. No, when he gets closer he sees it's not an old man but a youngish man—his age is hard to determine, but it can't be more than forty—with a mop of silver hair greased back. His frame is sturdy, and his thin spectacles are more like the kind of sunglasses that tint themselves when you walk outside. In one hand he holds a walking stick, idly twirling it as if practicing for a circus act.

Mickey knows this man is here for him, but he pretends not to notice. Instead he casts his gaze back and forth as if looking for the bus.

"Mickey Scarlet?"

Mickey turns to face the man. This time he notices that the stranger is skinny to the point of emaciation, and his slender, elegant fingers are curled around an ornate lion's head at the top of his walking stick. When he speaks his perfect teeth are wreathed with a set of thin lips that would have been at home on the Marquis de Sade's face. Though there is nothing menacing about this man, there is something that implies exceptional cruelty. He wears a fashionable raincoat, shiny dress boots and a decorative scarf. Mickey thinks he's rich, but why advertise something like that at a bus stop in front of a prison?

"Do I know you?" Mickey asks.

One corner of the man's mouth twists up in a crooked smile. "Not yet. But I'm quite familiar with you. My name is Lucifer Robinson." He holds out a limp hand.

Mickey takes it and is surprised by the strength the man uses to pump. There is wire in him. He's not just a foppish face. "Pleased to make your acquaintance."

Lucifer cocks his head, which makes his smile look even more warped. "I can see it on your face. You're wondering if that's my real name."

Mickey senses a rehearsed speech coming. Best to get it out of the way so they can get down to business. He keeps his mouth shut.

"It is. My mother was a staunch Catholic, and I was her first child. I was a bit late, and she didn't have very good birthing hips, so I quite literally tore my way into the world. It hurt her so much that she named me after the thing that scared her the most. She didn't live much longer after that. I suppose you could say she was the first person I ever killed."

Mickey remains silent.

Lucifer giggles like a pleased child. "Ah, you are difficult to shock! I think we've chosen very wisely." His gray eyes travel up and down Mickey's body before his entire face smiles. "You will most definitely do."

Mickey turns his back. "Not interested."

Lucifer steps around him and looks him in the eyes. "You haven't even heard what we have to offer."

Mickey turns again, hoping the bus will come soon.

Lucifer doesn't pursue him this time. Instead he leans on his walking stick. "You owe us, Mr. Scarlet. Who do you think got you out of prison so prematurely?"

"I kind of figured." Mickey doesn't look away from the road. "But I'm not interested in working for the mob."

Lucifer chuckles. It is a musical sound that echoes off the stone walls of the penitentiary. "It would be too easy to label us as the mob, Mr. Scarlet. We're even better."

Mickey's head swivels on his neck just far enough so he can see only a sliver of Lucifer. "Then who are you?"

"That doesn't matter. You'll probably find out someday. All that matters is, we're your future."

Mickey grunts. "I could have made it in

prison."

A distant roar signals the coming of the bus. Mickey squints and can see a gray oblong approaching on the road.

"So I heard. You made quite a reputation for yourself in that place. But I'd like to add that we were also responsible for making sure you didn't go down for murder one. Did you think your idiot lawyer managed that all on his own?"

"That makes no sense. If that was the case, why didn't you make *all* of the charges disappear? If you guys are such hot shit."

"Most of us weren't sure about you," Lucifer says. "We had to make sure you were made of the right stuff. After all those years in this place—" He hooks a thumb at the prison. "—we knew you were the man for us. Some of the things you got away with in there . . ." He mock shudders.

The bus pulls up, and the door slides open. Mickey steps up. "So long, Lucifer."

"Don't get on that bus. At least not without hearing me out. Okay?"

Mickey pauses, still holding the ticket. "What do you want me for?"

"I can't tell you everything, but I can give you a thumbnail sketch. Come with me."

Mickey stands with one foot on the bus and the other on the curb. The ticket grows soggy between his fingers and thumb. He stares at the silver-haired man, wondering. Would he spend the rest of his life regretting not at least listening to whatever pitch this man has in mind? What can they possibly want with him? And how much can he benefit? Most of all, why would anyone go through all this trouble just for him?

"You coming, pal?" The bus driver looks down from his heavenly perch, a fist on the handle that would close the door.

"What do you have waiting for you out in the world?" Lucifer asks. "You won't make it very far with that prison check in your pocket, and you don't even know where your family is. Come with me. At the very least you'll have something to occupy your time for a while. You'll be able to put together some money before you go find Melissa. What do you say?"

His mother named him well. Mickey really did have no idea where he was going. Maybe a motel room somewhere. How long would that last? What kind of work could he get? No one wanted to hire a multiple felon. And then there is Melissa and his child . . .

Too many questions boil in the stew of his brain. Sweat bubbles out of his skin, and his hands itch to hold an axe.

The bus driver looks at his watch. "I'm one minute ahead of schedule, my friend. That's how long you've got to make up your mind."

Mickey removes his foot from the bus and plants it next to the other on the pavement. "I'll get the next one."

The driver shrugs. "Good luck, son."

The door whisks shut, and a cloud of diesel smoke billows into the air as the bus roars off into the distance.

Lucifer smiles. "You've made a very sound decision."

Mickey doubts it. He remembers the old saying about the cat and what curiosity did to it. He hopes the other half of the saying, that satisfaction brought the feline back, isn't just piss in the wind.

CHAPTER THREE

Mickey follows the silver-haired man down the road for about a quarter-mile before they come upon a long white limo. The driver leans against the hood, smoking a cigarette. Most of his face is hidden by a chauffeur's hat, but not even the brim can conceal his bristly cheeks. The man's hands are the size of cannonballs. Mickey can tell that driving is just this man's day job; he is a pure, grade-A bruiser.

As soon as he sees his boss coming, the driver opens the back door, waiting. Lucifer wordlessly slides into the seat and all the way across, making room for his guest.

Mickey hesitates. He can see his distorted reflection in the driver's sunglasses. It makes him look wider and squat, almost like a dwarf.

Lucifer stows his walking stick next to his leg and picks up a glass of amber fluid from the armrest. He takes a sip and looks up at Mickey.

"Coming?"

Mickey can smell the sharp tang of whiskey on the man's breath. "Who are you? Really?"

Lucifer laughs. "I wish I could say that all will be revealed, but that's just not going to happen. If you come with me, you'll get some answers. Not all but some. Enough to keep you going. Care for a drink?"

Mickey looks back into the driver's face. There is no emotion here, just stoic patience.

Mickey gets in the car. He sees a line of seats opposite of Lucifer, so he sits there. For a moment he feels disoriented. Something isn't right about this limo. The back seat somehow seems bigger than the outside suggests.

Forget it. Must be my imagination.

"I'll have a whiskey," he says.

"I hope you like Johnnie Walker Blue," Lucifer says. He pours, no rocks.

Mickey takes the drink. The blue label has always been out of his price range. He sniffs it, but it doesn't smell unusual at all. He sips at it, and while it's good, it's nothing spectacular. Still, not bad for his first drink in years.

The driver closes the door without slamming it, and soon the limo eases forward and into traffic.

Mickey takes another drink, trying to ignore Lucifer's pale, unwavering gaze. He can't do it, no matter how long he stares into the tumbler. He can feel Lucifer's light blue eyes coring out his heart. No shadows fall upon his face, not even as the light shifts with the vehicle's movements. He merely shimmers like a ghost. Mickey can feel himself coming apart.

Lucifer's face breaks open into a smile. "First, I

want to tell you what you will get. Then we'll get to your reciprocation, and honestly it isn't much. In fact, a man like you could probably do this in his sleep."

Mickey waits.

"We're taking you to your new home right now. You will live in an apartment. It's a decent place. Not great but you won't have to fend off rats to get to the kitchen. It's a second-floor place with a bedroom, bathroom, kitchen and several roomy closets. Here are the keys."

Lucifer reaches into his pocket and places a ring of keys on the armrest well within Mickey's reach. When he does this, his movement is so smooth that the keys don't even jangle.

Mickey does not grab for them.

"Also on the ring you will find keys to your new car. Again, it isn't fancy, but it will get you from point A to point B without trouble. It's an old Chevy from the 'Eighties. It's a bit of a gas guzzler, but it's sturdy and nondescript.

"Your apartment will be stocked with the usual things people need to get by," Lucifer continues. "In the bathroom you'll find a shaving kit, toothbrush, comb and so on. In the bedroom you have a very comfortable bed with two goose-down pillows and silk sheets. In your living room you have a TV, a DVD player, internet and sufficient furniture. In your closet you will find clothes in the style you like, all in your size. We got your measurements from the prison doctor."

Mickey nods. This is supposed to impress him?

"In your kitchen you'll find a well stocked refrigerator as well as cupboards filled with plates and utensils and such. There is also a mighty fine collection of alcohol in the cabinet above the fridge. Most of it is whiskey, as that is your preferred beverage of choice."

"You've done your homework," Mickey says. "Good for you. But I don't—"

Lucifer holds up a delicate hand. "Please, Mr. Scarlet. Let me finish."

Mickey closes his mouth.

Lucifer removes a gold case from his pocket and selects a cigarette, which he eases between his thin lips. A gold lighter sparks, and smoke creeps throughout the vehicle. Surrounded by blue smoke, he looks more like a ghost than ever before.

He leans forward, his face spearing and separating the cloud around his head. "Every Friday you will receive two thousand dollars in your mailbox. You needn't worry about rent or car payments or anything important. This is just for you to do with as you wish. You have a job as a stock-boy in a grocery store, but you never have to go there. This is just in case someone asks."

"It sounds like you're setting me up for a life of leisure," Mickey says. "I believe the poets call that a charmed existence."

"I certainly hope so. I don't want you to feel any undue stress."

Mickey almost smiles at that. He searches Lucifer's face for any sign of humor, but it's hard to tell when someone always seems so mirthful.

"Every paradise has its snake," Mickey says. "What's the price?"

"It's quite simple. Every once in a while you'll be asked to perform a duty or task. Nothing serious. It won't put you out at all."

"What? Like bust a guy's kneecaps if he doesn't pay whoever you work for?"

Lucifer shrugs slightly, his grin crooked. "Well, there will be some of that. Considering your predilection for violence I don't think you would be opposed to it."

"Go on."

"There isn't much more to say. Just a yes or no, Mr. Scarlet."

Mickey wants to tell him no. To say yes would be like signing a blank check over to the devil. Despite everything that has happened over the past few years, he considers himself a good guy. Not great. He'd done too many questionable things to ever be considered great. He certainly isn't a hired thug, though. His deeds have always served a purpose, which isn't always to make him rich. Bottom line: for as much shit as he did in his life, the bad guys have always gone to prison. Is he to become someone's puppet?

But . . .

No.

"I'll have to say no. I don't mean to be a jag off and play with your name, but I'm not interested in deals with the devil."

"Heaven forbid playing with my name," Lucifer says. "The deal isn't with me, though. It's with my superior. And before you ask, his name is not Satan, Beelzebub, Mammon or anything along those lines."

"Then who are they?" Mickey asks. "I'm trying to figure out who would have a million bucks to waste getting me out of prison, just to turn me into an errand boy. And why me? There at least a hundred psychopaths in that prison who would jump at your offer."

"You said it yourself. They're psychopaths, and you're not."

Mickey's temples burn, and a cold trail of sweat slips down his back. "Are you sure about that?"

"Quite. You may have a short fuse, but that doesn't make you a psychopath. Psychopaths don't care about their wives and children like you do."

Mickey lunges across the backseat of the limo and wraps his hands up in Lucifer's lapels, yanking on them tightly enough to make his face start to glow red. "What the fuck do you know about Melissa?"

Lucifer smiles as the color spreads across his forehead. Mickey sees the veins pulsing behind Lucifer's papery skin. And then something prods into his belly. Mickey looks down and sees a gun in Lucifer's hand. It looks like nothing he's ever seen before. The barrel is a dragon, and the hole at the end is its mouth. Scales cover the pistol, and the beast's eyes seem to look directly up at Mickey.

"You think that scares me? Go ahead. Pull the fucking trigger."

Lucifer gags. "I have . . . no intention . . . of doing so." He coughs, and spittle flies from his lips. "I need . . . your services."

Mickey's fingers uncoil, and Lucifer gasps for air, loosening his tie with trembling fingers. He puts the safety on the gun and sets it aside, but not so far that he can't reach it if needed.

"You're not going to tell me who pulls your strings," Mickey says.

Lucifer shakes his head. He pours himself more Johnnie Walker Blue and downs it in one fast gulp.

"Are you going to at least tell me why you want me specifically?"

Lucifer straightens his outfit, slapping the wrinkles out of his lapels. "You have just the correct skill set we're looking for, Mr. Scarlet, and your knowledge of laws and how to get around them are indispensable. You will need to think on your feet often and prudently. Many times you will need to exercise your proficiency with violence. Are you beginning to see why you're such an important person?"

"You need a thug. Thugs are a dime a dozen."

"But not smart thugs. Besides your intelligence and store of knowledge, you also possess the all-important feature we seek: instinct. Or paranoia, if you wish."

"And your boss was willing to pay a million bucks to spring me," Mickey says.

"That's right."

Mickey's teeth lock up and grind so tightly that his head aches. "What if I say no?"

"You're under no obligation," Lucifer says. "I'll just ask Lotho to pull the limo over, and you'd get out and walk away. As to what happens after that, that's up to you. You'll probably find a bar somewhere, maybe a cheap motel, and if you're lucky, you'll drink yourself to death."

Mickey shakes his head. "People don't just throw a million dollars away. You're not making sense."

Lucifer's eyes twinkle above his shiny teeth. "There was never a risk. We knew you'd say yes."

"Did you."

Lucifer nods.

Mickey considers the life Lucifer suggested he would lead if he said no and knows it's bullshit. He'll never drink himself to death. He has too much to do. But without Lucifer's help, what will happen? Can he really see himself in a miserable nine-to-five and living in a shitty neighborhood while trying to find his family?

"I'll do it," Mickey says. "One condition: I get to quit whenever I want to, for whatever reasons."

Lucifer nods. "Whatever you think is best."

Mickey grabs the key ring and stuffs it into his pocket. "Take me home."

CHAPTER FOUR

It's a shit hole, a cyst on the neighborhood's ass. It's also serviceable. There are no junkies nodding off on the sidewalk, no bums with their red, chapped hands out and there isn't a single prostitute to be seen. There are ominous dark stains on the concrete, and through the open limo window Mickey can smell the distinct tang of piss.

"It's not so bad," Lucifer says. "I've been to worse places. Besides, everything is in working order. Our best men checked it over. The neighbors might be a little loud sometimes, but I don't think you'll be otherwise bothered. Look. There's your car."

Lucifer points, and Mickey sees a rusty brown Chevy. It's a boat, just the way they used to make cars. Nothing sleek about this model. Though it is obviously a piece of shit, Mickey can't help but be impressed. It reminds him of his father's car

45

way back when.

"It's not much," Lucifer says, "but we had mechanics go over it to make sure everything was running well. If not smoothly. I believe they call it a PM service."

Mickey nods. His uncle is a mechanic, and he'd learned quite a few things from the guy. He wonders whatever happened to Jack Scarlet, whether or not he is even still alive. He remembers thinking when he was a child that he'd much prefer to be Uncle Jack's son rather than his father's. Jack could be a tough son of a bitch, but he was never a *mean* son of a bitch. Maxwell Scarlet had that covered well enough for the both of them.

"I'll check on you every once in a while," Lucifer continues. "Whenever we need you to do something. Until then you are free to do as you please."

Mickey grunts. "One prison to another?"

"Never. Unless, of course, you had the key to your cell back at the penitentiary and could leave whenever you wanted . . . ?"

Lotho opens the door and waits, his face as stationary as a piece of paper. Mickey finishes his drink, barely registering the taste of the expensive whiskey. He leaves the glass in the cup holder and slides out into the street.

Lucifer reaches out, offering his hand. "Until next time, Mr. Scarlet."

Mickey stares at the hand. "I don't think we're friends, Mr. Robinson."

Lucifer withdraws the hand. "I think you may be right at that. Good day."

Lotho eases the door shut and strides to the

driver's door. Mickey wonders what would happen if he jabbed at one of the giant bruiser's pressure points. Something suggests that he wouldn't make it. The air around Lotho seems aware, as if he is connected entirely with his surroundings. He might not have eyes in the back of his head, but the breeze around him would notify him of any attack well in advance. Lucifer chose his guard well.

The giant begins stepping into the driver's seat, but Mickey holds up a hand. "Hey Lotho."

Lotho pauses, but he does not turn to face Mickey.

"What kind of a name is Lotho? I'm trying to place it, but I don't think I've ever heard it before."

Lotho removes his chauffeur's cap and turns his bald head slightly, only far enough to show three puckered knots of scar tissue on his forehead. There can be no mistaking what they are, but there are also no exit wounds on the other side.

"I was not born with it." The guard's voice is heavily accented, perhaps from eastern Europe. "Among my people there are folk tales of an unkillable man."

Mickey doesn't need to ask for the legend's name, and he doesn't need further explanation. Lotho must be able to read it on his face; he puts his hat back on and slips into the driver's seat like a snake on grease. The limo glides away, and Mickey can only imagine Lucifer's face behind the tinted windows. Mickey thinks he's smirking.

He approaches the door of the apartment building. The sidewalk under his feet is cracked, and weeds poke out their green heads from beneath. Nature yearns to take back this wretched mess.

The light over the door is broken, and glass is scattered about the porch. Paint peels off the wooden frame, but the plastic door seems pretty sturdy.

He tries several keys before the right one opens his way inside. The first thing he sees is a row of mailboxes. One of them has his name on it. According to the label, he lives in apartment C. After a cursory glance at the two doors on the first floor, he figures out C is on the second story.

He takes the steps slowly until he can see two more doors: C and D. The car keys are pretty easy to identify, and since he'd already learned which one opened the main door, the only remaining key has to be the one. He unlocks the door to his new home and steps into the gloom.

It doesn't smell bad. There is an antiseptic quality about it, almost like a hospital, and he decides Lucifer's men have been through here pretty well. Usually such a scent denoted a crime. Whenever he used to walk onto a scene and smell cleaning products, it was a five to one bet that someone had tried cleaning up blood or semen.

But there are no stains here. He wonders what would happen if he ran a blue light over the floor and walls, and then he decides that he doesn't want to know.

The living room is pretty standard. No decorations. Just sensible furniture and an entertainment center. He never really cared for TV or movies, but he looks forward to trying out some music on the sound system.

He finds a selection of DVDs and CDs and

flips through them. The former holds little interest, but the latter isn't bad. There are some good selections, but the methodology of whoever picked them speaks more of a scattergun approach. Lucifer and his boys don't know everything. This comforts Mickey slightly.

The bedroom offers a bed and a bookcase. He looks over the spines only to find a bunch of true crimes and some mystery novels. He'd taken up reading while in prison, but it isn't a thing he regularly enjoys.

The next stop is the kitchen. There are steaks and burgers in the fridge, as well as a bunch of good beer and cheese. The staples of his diet. He finds the hard liquor in the cabinet as suggested by Lucifer. Good stuff. Nice selection. He takes down a bottle and tries to break the seal with his thumbnail. He can't get it in deep enough, so he uses his keys. As soon as the cork is out, he smells the amber spirits within.

He is tempted to drink from the bottle, but since he has glasses, why not drink like a civilized man? He takes a tumbler down from the cabinet and pours two fingers of whiskey. Considers. Pours two more. He takes the bottle with him when he goes back to the living room and sits down in his recliner. It is very comfortable, and he immediately feels at ease.

Mickey puts the cool glass to his lips and takes a sip. His mouth lights up with flame as his guts are kindled in the stove of his stomach. It is his second drink in years, and it goes straight to his head. He leans back and lets out a sigh. This isn't paradise, but after incarceration it is a suitable substitute.

This time he takes a gulp and lets his head float softly above his neck. The remote control rests by his hand, but he is in no way inclined to turn on the television, not even for the news.

There is just one thing missing, and when his palms twitch, he knows he can't live without it. There are trees even in this paradise.

He throws off the rest of the glass and leaves it on the coffee table. Once in the hallway again, he locks the door behind him. When he realizes what he's done, he almost laughs. It's not like this stuff is actually his. So what if someone steals it?

Locking up is so engrained in him that he can't help but do it. It's funny, feeling like a citizen again.

Mickey gets to the bottom of the stairs, and he opens the mailbox. There is an envelope with money in it, just as Lucifer promised. He stuffs it unopened into his pocket.

The car is comfortable inside, though it smells slightly like cigarettes, as if the person who had delivered it smoked heavily. The engine turns over easily, and when he drives the vehicle doesn't rattle or hum or anything. For all its rust on the exterior, the interior is a smooth ride, like a middle-aged whore. She might not look like much, but she can work a dick like no one's business.

Though this is a different part of town than he'd known, it isn't difficult finding a hardware store. He wanders around inside for a while before he finds what he is looking for. It doesn't resemble his old companion, but when he hefts the axe in both hands, he knows they are meant to know each other. The handle is smooth plastic. It is much sturdier than the splintered wood of his former axe. The head is heavier, too, but the blade looks honed enough to split a hair from end to end.

The implement hums in his hands, as if it is alive. It almost breathes. Already it feels like an extension of his body.

Balm in Gilead. Balm in fucking Gilead.

Mickey walks up to the counter. "How much?"

CHAPTER FIVE

The drive home is comfortable. It makes Mickey feel better to have the axe on the seat next to him. It radiates power, and he can feel an electric hum go up his arm when he touches it, just to remind himself that it is there.

He parks his new car in front of his new apartment, and carrying his new axe, he makes his way inside and up the stairs. He pauses just outside his door and cradles the implement like a baby. Comfort warms his belly, just as he'd expected, but it is so much more overwhelming than usual. It's like two companions rejoined after so many years.

Mickey opens the door, and he contemplates where he should put the axe. Back in the old days, he kept it in his car, but now he wants to keep it a lot closer to him, especially since he's on his own. Perhaps the closet?

No.

The coffee table next to his recliner? He anticipates spending a lot of time there, so it would probably be good to have it close at hand.

No. There is only one place where he should keep it. He goes to his bedroom and props it up next to his night table. It feels right. The room seems to be in utter harmony.

The phone rings, bringing cacophony to Mickey's ordered peace. He grimaces and goes to the living room, where a phone is hooked up near the front closet. It's on a table of its own, and it is old fashioned. A candlestick phone with a separate piece for the ear.

Just like the one his father had owned. How has he not noticed this before?

He picks it up and lifts the handle, putting it to his ear with his left hand. He aims his mouth at the piece in his other hand. "Hello?"

Silence. Maybe some ambient noise in the background. The ticking of a clock? The hum of some machinery? He can't tell what it is.

"Is there someone there?" he asks.

"Yes, you son of a bitch." The voice is unfamiliar, but it is sharp and vehement, like an angry witch's cackle. "You piece of shit. You'd better believe someone is here."

"Who the fuck is this?"

The voice on the other end laughs. There is no humor in it. Vitriol drives it through the phone lines.

"Fuck you," Mickey says. He hangs the ear piece back in place and sets down the phone, almost expecting it to ring again.

It doesn't.

The sense of harmony in this apartment is gone,

and there is nothing Mickey can do about it. He goes to the kitchen and pours himself more whiskey. He downs it in one go, but it doesn't make him feel any better.

CHAPTER SIX

On the second night in his new home, Mickey rests in bed, one arm behind his head and the other across his chest, watching the ceiling fan slowly rotate over him. At first he isn't aware of the sound coming through the wall, but eventually it becomes so loud that he recognizes it for what it is: an argument. Between a man and a woman. There is a child crying in the background.

It's none of his business. Lucifer warned him that the neighbors could get rowdy. He should have expected something like this. He tries to ignore it.

He hears the crack of flesh meeting flesh. The woman yelps, and the man shouts more.

Mickey sits up in bed, and in his closet he sees some kind of movement, like maybe rats trying to scurry away before being noticed. He stands and walks to the door, opening it all the way. There is something moving behind the hanging clothes, and he pushes them aside.

There are two figures in there, both very familiar. His father, a pulsing red hole just above his eyes, the back of his head blown out, revealing the tiny scrim of brains he has left. He towers over the crouching figure of Mickey's mother, and he slaps her back and forth across the face. There are horrible marks around her throat from where his old man had strangled her. Blood oozes from her split lip. She cries out for help, but no one is there except for Mickey. He remembers the day well. He remembers cowering in the hallway, unable to help because he was only five years old. All he can do is scream for his father to stop.

Mickey squeezes his eyes shut until they burn under his lids. When he opens them, his parents are gone, and he can still hear the struggle next door.

None of his business. He is no hero. What can he do?

He hears a meatier thump and the whistle of someone's breath leaving their body very quickly. A gut-punch, probably delivered so that the woman couldn't go around advertising the darkness of her husband's soul.

Mickey pushes himself away from the closet and strides to the front door. He wears only his boxers, but he never considers getting dressed. The beast is in his throat and pulling his strings. Even if wants to, there is no turning back.

He hammers on the door to apartment D. Cop-knock, as his old partner used to call it. It never fails to give a perp The Fear.

The shouts from behind the door cease. The locks unclick, and the chain rattles away before the door whips open. The man standing across the threshold is tall, maybe six-four, and he is covered with writhing muscles. The only soft part of him is his belly, and judging from the stink on his breath, it is the result of too much cheap beer. His brow juts out below a sloping forehead, and Mickey wonders, way back in his mind where he is still his own person, if the Neanderthals really had died out or not.

Something moves at their feet, and Mickey sees the man's shadow is flickering, almost as if he isn't really there. Mickey looks back up and sees the man's hair has turned into a mass of swaying tentacles, even the mustache under his nose. Something glows in the backs of his eyes, almost like a cat's.

The man's hand holds the door, and Mickey can see blood on his scarred knuckles. It runs down and twists, trying to dance away from him.

"What the fuck do you want?" The words slip through his jagged teeth and flop out on the floor like fish out of water. His mouth is smeared with something that wants to drool away.

Mickey has a catalogue of things he wanted to say, but the beast doesn't let him. His right hand darts out, jabbing two fingers into the upside down triangle at the base of the man's throat. The man tries to shield the blow, but the beast is too fast. Instead he grabs his throat, gagging as he tries to draw breath.

Mickey catches him by a clump of greasy hair, and even though it moves against his grip, Mickey manages to yank the man's head down into a knee. Something snaps in the man's face, and blood patters on the floor. The shadow is now straight and regular, and the glow has gone out of his eyes. There is nothing unusual about him anymore.

Mickey is about to stomp on the man's head when he sees that the man isn't moving. The beast retreats, and Mickey feels fear stab him in the belly. He almost reaches down to check for a pulse, but then he hears the rattling wheeze of breath, and the wife-beater is moving slightly. Unconscious but moving.

Mickey's palm crawls with the grease from the man's hair, and he feels the immediate need to wash it away. He looks up from the pile of human refuse at his feet. A woman stands about three yards away, staring at him through a pair of eyes so black she could be a raccoon. Snot cakes her nostrils shut, and she holds both hands closely to her breasts. Peeking out from around the leg of her nightgown is a boy of about five. They both stare at him as if expecting him to say something, to perhaps explain himself.

"Try to keep it down, okay?" he says. He instantly wishes he had kept his mouth shut. His words sound too cold even to his own ears, and he knows that he'd beaten this man down for more than just enough peace to go to sleep.

Neither wife nor child say a word.

Mickey goes back to his apartment, where he washes his hands with a dollop of dishwasher. When he is sure he has scrubbed enough, he grabs a bottle of whiskey and pours a few fingers. He takes the drink to bed where he sips at it and watches the ceiling fan turn.

His neighbor would not let this go. No, Mickey would see that son of a bitch again, of this he is certain.

He tosses off the remainder of his drink and tries to sleep. Instead he thinks about the beast.

CHAPTER SEVEN

The next day, Mickey is bored so he starts reading one of the paperback books that had been left for him in his apartment. He finds it surprisingly entertaining, and he's so engrossed with it that he nearly misses it when his doorbell rings. He doesn't bother to check who it is; he just buzzes them in and waits by his open front door.

Lucifer Robinson slowly makes his way up the stairs, not bothering with the railing. He leans on his walking stick as he goes. Behind him lumbers Lotho, still wearing his sunglasses even though the hallway is slightly dim on an overcast day.

"Mr. Scarlet," Lucifer says. "I hope you're finding your accommodations to your satisfaction."

"It's not bad," Mickey says. "Come on in. Want a drink?"

Lucifer steps past him, digging into his coat for his flask. "No thank you. I brought my own." He flashes silver, shaking it so a dancing reflection of light illuminates the wall, before he puts it into his side pocket.

"How about you, Lotho?"

"He doesn't drink," Lucifer says.

Mickey goes to the kitchen and takes down a bottle of whiskey. He pours. "Sit where you like." Even though Lucifer probably already had.

When Mickey comes back to the living room, he sees Lucifer has perched himself on the couch, and he is examining the book Mickey has been reading. His cursory glance shows that he's not actually reading anything.

Lotho stands off to the side, not moving.

"You probably know why I'm here," Lucifer says. He places the book back on the coffee table, face down and open to the page where Mickey had left off.

"Yeah. What's my first job?"

"It's quite simple. You are to pick up a package and deliver it for us."

"Just like that?" Mickey laughs. "You sprang me from the joint just so I could be your errand boy?"

"I told you, your tasks would be very easy."

Mickey drinks. "Details."

*

The instructions are so simple no one can screw them up, not even the most nervous rookie. Mickey knows it's so idiot-proof because it's a test. Fine. He can follow instructions.

The hardest part of it is the neighborhood. The docks are a very tough place. Scarred fisherman and bristling butchers populate the seafront. Some of them have been at their mean jobs for so long they no longer look human. Their eyes are wider than they should be. Missing limbs have been replaced by hooks and other contraptions. In the gray light and the mist coming off the water, some of them seem to be ghosts. See-through shapes moving in the cloudy obfuscation. Foghorns bellow and boats groan.

Mickey knows that if he doesn't look tough, he's in trouble. He keeps up his usual demeanor, the one he always wore while haunting the meanest streets in the city as a cop, and no one bothers him. No one so much as challenges his steely gaze.

He finds the store easily enough. The address is clearly labeled, and he doubts there are any other places around here named Melville's Cleaver. When Lucifer told him about it, Mickey had taken it for a reference to the author of *Moby-Dick*. Much to his surprise, a sign on the wall proclaims this place to be owned by a man named Nathan Melville.

The area of the store where the customers are received is pretty clean. There are droplets of blood sprinkled all over the tile floor, but aside from this it is spotless enough to be featured on a postcard. From the counter on back, however, is a different story. The cash register, an old fashioned one with no digital readout and a series of dingy numbers on popup tabs, is smudged with blood and dirt. The scale has a coagulated lump on it. Flies crawl across it in droves. A wall of hanging meat separates the front of the store from the back, where the real work undoubtedly occurs.

Some of it Mickey can identify as fish, from a six-incher all the way up to a full-sized shark. Other pieces are not quite so easily recognized. Dead eyes gazed back at him by the dozen. Some of these fish don't look like fish should. Some of them have extra fins. One of them has fingers.

Thunk! The sound drifts from the back room, and very shortly thereafter it comes again.

Mickey steps up to the counter where a desk bell waits. It is greasy with something, but he doesn't care to try to identify it. He rings it using the back of a fingernail, and he still wipes it clean on his pants.

The curtain of fish splits apart, and a tall fat man emerges. What little hair he has is slicked back, and his beard is long and straggly. It all sways slightly, and Mickey thinks they might be bunches of tentacles. The man has giant eyes, and they are slanted slightly. There is a vague Asian feeling about him, but it's all thrown off by the scars just below his face. It looks like several attempts had been made to slit his throat. They failed, of course, but none of them seem to stretch across the length of his throat, only under each side of his skull like gills. The apron he wears around his waist might have once been white, but it will never be again. Blood has had its way with it. Still, his name is clear on the breast: MELVILLE.

He is holding a giant cleaver, and blood runs up and down its length. He places it down on the counter and wipes sweat from his high forehead with the back of his monstrously large hand. At first it looks like he might have a flipper instead, but upon closer examination, Mickey sees that the butcher is missing a couple of fingers.

"What do you want?" He has a vague accent. It is not easy for Mickey to place.

Not that he needs to. Time for the script. "I'm a bit parched from walking around. You got any rum?"

Melville's response is perfect: "This look like a fuckin' bar to you?"

"I guess I'll just have water, then."

Melville nods. "That, I got."

He ducks beneath the counter and pulls out a label-less bottle as if he is living in a western. Two shot glasses join the bottle next to the scale. The butcher turns his back and pushes the fish aside again. Mickey gets the message. He pours them each a drink. The glasses are a lot cleaner than anything else in here, which makes him feel better.

While he waits for Melville to return, he sniffs at the booze and nearly recoils. If it hadn't been so dark, he might have taken it for turpentine.

The butcher returns bearing a package that looks like any other that would have come from this shop. It is wrapped in wax paper like a piece of meat and is as long as one's forearm. He slips it into a brown paper lunch bag and folds the top closed.

Mickey reaches into his pocket and pulls out a wad of hundred dollar bills. Pinching it between his ring and pinkie fingers, he offers it to the butcher. Melville snaps it away and leaves the package on the counter.

"Thank you for the water," Mickey says.

Melville nods, thus ending the performance. He reaches for one of the shot glasses and takes down the drink. Mickey follows suit. The horrible concoction sets his mouth on fire, and he feels like puking up whatever the fuck he'd just drunk. He forces the thought from his mind. Showing weakness is not just a bad idea in this neighborhood, but it would also reflect poorly on Lucifer's bosses, whoever they may be.

Mickey forces himself to swallow, and the wretched drink fills his belly like cement. Flames seem to bellow from the back room, and everything has a red outline. Melville grins at him, showing off a mouthful of jagged, sharp teeth. Meat clings between them, and blood oozes from the corners of his mouth and eyes. Something flies across Mickey's vision. A bird? He can't tell. There are ants everywhere, crawling all over his shoes and hands. They march their way out of the bottle of rotgut and rest in the bottom of both shot glasses.

Mickey closes his eyes and squeezes them tightly. He counts to five and opens them, cocking his head to the side. Everything is calm now. No ants. Nothing flying in the store.

He blows his breath out. "That's strong. What was that?"

Melville smiles, and his teeth are still jagged, but none of them are sharp. They're just rotten. "It's a shit shot. You take the worst whiskey you can find, the foulest tequila you can find and the nastiest vodka you can find, and you pour it all into a bottle in equal parts."

"That's a hard drink." But Mickey doesn't think that's all there is to it.

"Hard as they fucking come." And Melville winks, as if confirming Mickey's suspicions.

*

Back in his car, Mickey wonders if maybe he should open the package just to see what business Lucifer is into. Smelling it reveals nothing but a fishy odor. No wonder, considering where it had come from. However, the wrapping is so intricate that he doesn't think he'd be able to put it back together.

Maybe that's the test.

It has to be drugs of some sort. It's definitely some kind of smuggling job, since he'd made the pickup at the seafront. Melville is slightly Asian. Is it opium?

He drops the package on the passenger seat. He's thinking too much like a cop. He can't do that anymore. Just let it go. The job is what's important. Nothing else should figure in.

Mickey drives across town to a fairly decent neighborhood. Not so bad that he has to look down or look tough, but not so good that he'll stick out. He finds the apartment he is looking for, so he gets out and looks for the correct doorbell. Lucifer has told him the name would be Papoulos, and there it is, the second from the top. He presses the button and waits.

The speaker clicks. "Who goes?"

Mickey falls back into the script. "Courier for Mr. John Quint."

"You've got the wrong address," comes the expected reply. "What address you lookin' for?"

"210C," Mickey says.

"Nah, this is 210B, but I know the guy. He's my neighbor. I'll buzz you in."

A grinding sound that might have once been a buzzer blares, and the door unlocks. Mickey walks in and goes up the stairs to the correct door.

A skinny white kid stands over the threshold, dressed only in a robe. His blond hair goes down to his shoulders in a ragged mess, and his blue eyes are just about as empty as a human being's can get.

The kid probably hadn't bathed in a month, but even stronger than his rancid BO is the bitter reek of smoke. Not gentle enough for cannabis, not sharp enough for meth. Once again, Mickey guesses: opium.

"Where should I leave Mr. Quint's package?" he asks.

"I'll take it." Papoulos holds out a bony hand on a stalk of pale, thick-veined arm.

Mickey catches a glimpse of a young girl through the crack in the door. Maybe too young. She is skinnier than Papoulos, and for a moment, Mickey thinks that she has an extra eye on her face.

It takes him a moment to realize that she has *two faces*, but they both share the same mouth and nose. One side stares off into space, possibly dead. The other watches Papoulos's hand, eager for whatever Mickey has.

Mickey hands over the package, and Papoulos reciprocates with a bulging envelope. Without looking inside, Mickey stuffs it into his jacket pocket.

"Make sure he gets it," he says.

"This very night." So ends the script.

Mickey looks back to the two-faced girl, and she seems so happy it nearly breaks his heart.

Papoulos closes the door.

And that is it.

*

As Mickey steps up to his apartment building, the money weighing half of his jacket down, he sees a boy playing outside in the grass. He waves a bunch of army men around through the thicket. The dolls are nothing fancy, just little plastic green men.

As he approaches, the kid looks up. Mickey recognizes him as the boy next door. The last he'd seen of the lad was a sliver of face poking out from behind his mother.

It looks like the boy wants to say something, but Mickey turns his attention away. He works the key in the door, but he can feel the kid's eyes on his back. His neck hair stands up a little. He steps inside, but he can't help but look back.

The boy is still sitting in the grass, but the soldiers in his hands have been forgotten. He watches Mickey with a look of wonderment, perhaps even fear. The biggest monster the kid has ever known is his father, and Mickey has pounded the shit out of him.

Yeah, it's probably fear.

CHAPTER EIGHT

The next day is overcast, too, and it is dark by seven o'clock. Mickey walks up to his building with an armful of groceries. It doesn't take much to keep him fed. Just some burger patties, a couple of steaks and a shitload of potato chips. Booze is another story. Now that he has so much money on hand, he is able to experiment a little. He usually kept to the cheap shit with a good bottle for special occasions. Now he has a little of everything, and each sample costs more than thirty bucks each. The bottles clink against each other in a brown paper bag, under which he has a careful, guarded hand.

He approaches the front door to the building, and the hair on the back of his neck dances. A cloud floats over his brain. His body tenses, and he looks around, unsure. Something isn't right, but he can't tell what. He trusts his instincts. They kept him alive for many years. This is the sensation he gets when someone near to him intends him violence.

He sees no one.

He doesn't relax. Instead he slows his pace. He tries to look casual.

The porch light has been repaired, but it is not on yet. The streetlights blaze behind him, so his shadow is splashed across the door, but it is almost too dark to see the keyhole. There is some comfort in this shadow. Mickey now knows that whoever tries to sneak up on him will have their presence broadcast before them.

He places the bags on the ground and fishes around in his pocket, making a show of it, keeping a watchful eye on the door in front of him.

Something scuffs on the sidewalk behind him, and it is followed by another similar sound. It is slow enough to suggest someone is creeping along.

Mickey pulls out his key ring and pretends to be looking for the right one, holding it up to the light from behind him. The person's footsteps come closer, and another shadow spreads in front of him.

Is this another test from Lucifer Robinson? Perhaps an old enemy? No. The wind picks up a little, and Mickey can smell whiskey breath and BO. He knows who this is.

He whips around and hurls his keys into his neighbor's face, catching him on the forehead. He yelps with surprise, and the baseball bat he is holding clatters to the sidewalk.

Mickey doesn't give him time to recover. He scoops up the bat and jabs the thick end into his neighbor's gut, doubling the greasy asshole over. The neighbor blows out a lungful of halitosis so hard it nearly makes Mickey gag.

Mickey had wanted this to be a quick lesson, and for a while he thinks he's in charge of this situation. All he wanted to do was beat the bastard a bit and send him on his way, but the beast suddenly takes the reigns.

Mickey can't stop himself from clubbing his neighbor on the back of his scraggly head. There is a line-drive crack, and his neighbor goes down in a pile of his own stink.

Mickey kicks him several times in the side. When he starts, he wants to make sure the bastard is really down, but it slowly turns into something fun to do.

And then Mickey notices his neighbor's partner. This guy is skinny with a head of stringy dark hair. He wears a leather vest and has a sleeve of tats up both arms. Dragons and barbed wire. He holds a butterfly knife in one work-gnarled hand.

His eyes are frisbees, and his mouth looks like a fish's. Loose, aged flesh jiggled, and a wet spot formed at the crotch of his pants.

Mickey points the fat end of the bat at him. "Are you gonna stop me?"

The partner looks down at the knife in his own tremulous hand, then back at Mickey. Indecision. Mickey steps forward to help the process along, but the man is too rooted in place to fear the sudden movement.

Mickey snarls and lashes out with the bat, knocking the butterfly knife from the man's hand. It clatters up the street, where it skitters into a storm drain.

This time the man jumps so hard his hair flies almost into an imitation of an afro, and he stumbles backwards, eager to escape.

Mickey doesn't pay any more attention to him. The guy is fleeing, and that is the important thing. Time to get back to his neighbor.

The bastard is out cold, lying on the concrete like a beached whale. He whistles when he breathes, and to Mickey it sounds like fingernails on a chalkboard. He wants nothing more than to end that horrible noise.

He pauses over the man's head and feels his arms lifting the bat up to the sky. Somewhere inside of his mind he knows he shouldn't be doing this, but he is no longer in the driver's seat. This is the beast's gig, and it knows how to handle things on a permanent basis.

Mickey glances up to see the baseball bat over his head, and he sees the neighbor's wife at the window of their apartment. She stares down at him, but she doesn't say a word. Is she giving him permission to do this? Or is she just too scared to do anything?

Shame creeps into his belly like a whining dog, and the beast retreats. The energy drains from his arms, and they drop to his side. The bat jangles on the sidewalk and rolls away into the grass.

Mickey looks up to the neighbor's wife, and her demeanor doesn't change. She now holds a phone to her ear, but her facial features are the same. He can barely read 911 in her eyes.

Shit.

If he's going to have a talk with cops, he'd rather wait for them in the comfort of his own home. He rolls his neighbor over so he can get his keys out from under the sweaty flab, and he picks up his groceries.

It takes them a half an hour to arrive. Not to talk with Mickey, but to *arrive*. In that time he has prepared a couple of burgers and is drinking beer. He sits by the window so he can watch. The flashing lights announce their presence, and soon they are giving his neighbor a once over.

One of them picks up the baseball bat and nods to his partner. As they approach the door to the apartment building, his neighbor's scuzzy partner shows up and starts rambling. He isn't loud enough for Mickey to hear, but he has no doubt the idiot is spilling his guts. The entire stupid story with him as an accomplice to his friend's intent to commit battery.

Mickey shakes his head, thinking about what the stupid fuck is admitting to. From the look on the one cop's face, he can't believe what he's hearing. Before the idiot finishes babbling, he is cuffed and stuffed into the back of the cruiser.

The paramedics arrive, and they go to work on the neighbor. The cops go inside, presumably to talk with his neighbor's wife.

The burgers are ready, so Mickey grabs another beer and digs in. It might be a while before his interrogation, so he might as well go into it well fed.

Soon the neighbor is cleaned off the sidewalk and packed away into an ambulance. About that time, someone knocks on Mickey's door. Cop knock. He finishes off his food and ambles to the door.

He is surprised to discover that he actually knows one of the officers. Travis Gerald looks a bit older, and he has a little less hair at the temples, but his baby face is still the same as ever. Mickey is about to express this when he notices Travis's stationary face. There is no recognition there.

There is also something else odd about the cops. It takes Mickey a moment, but he notices that neither of them are casting shadows. He looks down at his own feet and sees a puddle of darkness. They should have shadows.

"Mr. Scarlet?" Travis asks. There is nothing unusual about his voice, no wink of the eye, nothing to show that he is just pretending not to know who Mickey is.

"Sure. What can I do for you?"

"I'm Officer Gerald, and this is my partner Officer Gould. We'd like to ask you a few questions."

Mickey steps aside. "Come in. You want a beer?"

"No thanks," Gould says.

"You sure? I got some Schlitz in the fridge."

Finally. Travis's façade breaks down a bit. Mickey has no Schlitz, but he knows it is Travis's drink of choice.

The officer refuses to meet his eyes. "No thank you."

The interview is short. He learns that his neighbor's name is Arvin Jakowski, and they ask him for his version of the story. He gives them the truth. They want to know what could have possibly caused this incident, and Mickey explains about the previous incident a few nights ago.

Neither officer takes down notes.

"Thank you, Mr. Scarlet, for your time," Travis says. "You'll be contacted by a detective shortly for a follow-up interview."

Travis and Gould head for the door. Just before Travis makes his exit, Mickey holds up a finger. "Is there really going to be a follow-up interview?"

Travis doesn't turn. "Sir?"

"What's with all this Mr. Scarlet bullshit? You and I know each other. We've played poker, shot pool, all that wonderful shit. What's up, Travis?"

The officer turns. "Have a good day, sir."

And he's gone.

Mickey bolts the door and thinks about Lucifer Robinson.

And no, there is no follow-up interview.

CHAPTER NINE

Lucifer sits on the couch, smoking a cigarette and relaying the information for a new pickup and delivery. Mickey says, "Never mind that shit for now. We have something else to talk about."

Lucifer pauses in mid-sentence, and the corner of his mouth turns up. "I assume you mean Arvin Jakowski."

Mickey nods.

Lucifer reaches for his flask and takes a belt from it. The acrid stink of his breath wafts over to Mickey. "What about him?"

"The police report's been wiped, hasn't it?"

"I don't follow, Mr. Scarlet."

Mickey feels the urge to grab a handful of Lucifer's pretty-boy hair and yank it down so hard his nose would break against the edge of the coffee table. But he restrains himself.

"You mean the altercation," Lucifer says.

"Yes. The one with the baseball bat."

"I hear it was rather gruesome. Then again I hear Mr. Jakowski's a wife abuser. I disapprove of working out one's aggression on the weaker sex."

Mickey grunts. "Lucifer Robinson. Man of mystery and champion of feminism."

"Undoubtedly. Are you asking me if you are suddenly above the law?"

Mickey hesitates. He wouldn't have put it quite that way, but that is exactly what he'd meant. "I guess so. Do I have *carte blanche* to run amok?"

Lucifer laughs. "No. It took some serious money to cover up last night's events. We're more than happy to make any small indiscretions disappear, but we don't have an endless supply of money. I'm sure my superiors would frown upon further vigilantism. I advise you to leave Arvin Jakowski as your final act of unsanctioned violence."

"Right," Mickey says. "Did I pass your test?"

Lucifer stares at him for a moment, and his poker face is a cement block, unmoving and impenetrable. "I fear the mystery of your situation has started having an effect on your perception. You're starting to see plots where there are none. I suggest you forget about it and concentrate on your next job."

"Another pickup and delivery in a long boring string of pickups and deliveries? I thought you said my more violent nature would come into play at some point."

"Eventually," Lucifer says. "For the time being, we have other uses for you. Besides, are you so eager to shed blood so soon after Arvin Jakowski?"

Mickey honestly doesn't know. Thinking back on the incident makes him feel a little ill. If he hadn't seen Mrs. Jakowski at the window, he would most certainly have killed her husband. The prospect doesn't appeal much to Mickey, but the beast? It still stirs in the depths of his heart. It wants blood and death, and though it is calm for now, he has doubts that he's seen the last of it.

Lucifer must have read it all on his face. When Mickey comes back to himself, the pallid man smiles and twiddles with his cigarette. "I didn't think so. If it's any consolation to you, these tiny jobs are designed to place you in a position for something bigger. You'll see."

Lucifer continues giving Mickey the details.

*

It's Melville again, and Mickey is getting used to the shit shot. It is absolute swill, and he doesn't think it's a good sign that he's becoming accustomed to it.

Melville seems pleased with him, though. The butcher never smiles, but he nods with approval by their fifth meeting. The script is now lax and unnecessary. They trust each other, and that is enough for Melville.

Mickey takes the package to Papoulos, who is not quite as trusting. Last time he'd invited Mickey in to try some of the product and perhaps one of his women, and Mickey had respectfully declined. Not respectfully enough, apparently, as Papoulos continues to insist on the script. There are never any pleasantries, not that Mickey gives much of a shit. It's a job.

Today it's heroin. Mickey knows this because Melville says so. He isn't surprised to see a couple of fixing junkies jittering on the floor behind Papoulos. Both look like they'll never see their fifteenth birthday. Their skin is sloughing off their bodies and melting into the floor. Their bones are so sharp they seem to be cutting their way out of their bodies. One of them whispers something, but it is inaudible through his chattering teeth.

Papoulos catches Mickey looking at the junkies. "Don't fucking judge me."

Is he judging Papoulos? Mickey doesn't know, but if he is he certainly has no business doing it. He thinks back to all the smack he'd helped run on the streets when he was a cop. It was a hell of a paycheck. The cocaine had helped buy his house in the boonies, but smack was and is a popular hit and very much in demand.

But something eats at the back of his mind. Not the beast. Guilt? Indignation? What?

"I'm not judging anyone, kid. It's none of my business."

The door closes, and Mickey remains standing there for a while, lost in the whorls and swirls in the wood grain. He looks at it long enough to see the pattern of two eyes, one larger than the other, a cavernous nose and a screaming, agonized mouth. This last is right by the door knob.

It blinks, and the mouth turns up into a grin. The door puffs out a little, like a man taking a breath, and Mickey turns away from it.

*

When Mickey gets home, he does something he doesn't usually do: he turns on the television and watches some program or another. The content doesn't matter to him. He stares past the images until he can see the individual pixels. He deconstructs the image so much that he can't see the whole anymore.

Melissa and his child. What does the kid look like? Is it a boy or a girl? Probably a boy with all of his mother's looks. Somehow Mickey can't envision himself with a daughter. One sex or the other, the kid wouldn't look like him. He's too ugly, and he doesn't wish that on anyone.

He's tried looking for Melissa, but he can't find a way to contact her. The prison refuses to give out her address, and he can't find her in the phone book. The day before he'd spent some time on Facebook trying to find her that way. Nothing. Isn't everyone supposed to have a Facebook page? He thinks maybe she has a private account.

Part of him wants to ask Lucifer for help, but he doubts he would get an answer.

No, Mickey has to try something else. There is only one way this can go: he has to contact an expert. Someone who is discreet and maybe a little unscrupulous. Most importantly this person couldn't be known by Lucifer or any of his people.

Mickey goes through the catalogue of private investigators in his mind. Most cops don't like gumshoes, but Mickey used them often back when he was on the force. Whenever he needed something investigated off the books, or when his face was too public for it, he went to his rolodex where he had a list of PI's who worked in gray areas.

He no longer has that rolodex, but he figures Willie Salas is slimy enough for this job. The guy is cheap, and he knows how to think around corners. Provided, of course, that the creepy bastard is still alive.

Mickey turns off the TV and reaches for a bottle of whiskey. It is too late to give Willie a visit, and Mickey is too keyed up with thoughts of finally seeing his family again to go to sleep, so he needs a bit of help from the kindest spirit of them all: amber.

The candlestick phone rings. He stares at it while it rings a second time. He knows it's his prank caller, and he doesn't want to talk to them. But when it rings an eighth time, he knows it's not going to stop. He stands and goes to the cord. He pulls it from the wall.

The phone rings again. And again. And again.

Mickey picks up the ear piece. "Hello?"

Laughter. Cruel and empty. "Fuck you, Mickey Scarlet."

"You piece of shit. Who is this?"

"Fuck you. Fuck you. Fuck you."

Mickey slams the ear piece back into its cradle. He almost expects the phone to ring again. He is relieved when it doesn't.

INTERLUDE

"Are you sure about this?"

Travis shrugs. "I know how it sounds, but that's what I saw."

There is a toothpick in Karnaki's mouth, and he bites down on it so hard he splinters the tip. "That's not possible. Mickey Scarlet is rotting in prison. He's not even up for parole for, what, five years?"

"I'm telling you what I saw," Travis says. "You can ask Gould if you want. He was there."

"And it was for some kind of domestic disturbance?"

Travis moves a flat hand like it's a boat on a stormy sea. "Kinda. Mickey beat the shit out of a guy who was trying to sneak up on him. Revenge thing. From what I understand Mickey beat the shit out of him before. Thought he'd get a buddy and give Mickey a surprise."

"Why didn't you arrest him? That's what you

should have done."

Travis squirms just a little bit. His shirt collar suddenly seems too tight. He grabs at it and pulls a little. He realizes what he's just done, and he hopes Karnaki doesn't notice.

He does. "Answer my question, officer. What, are the two of you friends from way back when? You decided to cut him a break."

"It's not like that. And yes, we used to hang out together in the old days. But that's not it at all."

"Then what?" Karnaki holds up both of his meaty hands, palms up, exasperated.

"It, uh, came from high up. No one does nothing to Mickey."

"High up?" Karnaki tries to think of what this even means. Though he's a federal agent, and Travis is a street cop, he can't imagine any situation in which a higher up would let a violent incident pass without an arrest being made.

"Look, I don't know how to explain this to you, man. You're pretty close to this Mickey Scarlet thing. You busted him back in the day, right?"

Karnaki nods.

"Then you're probably going to find out for yourself. I can't really tell you how it is. It's . . . it's too difficult."

Karnaki nods again. "All right. I'm going to talk to your superiors. I worked goddam hard on putting that piece of shit behind bars, and I want him to stay there for the duration."

"Go ahead. Talk to everyone up to the commissioner. I guarantee you'll get the same story I'm giving you. They're not going to be able to explain it to you, either. And maybe they shouldn't."

"We'll see."

*

Karnaki doesn't have time to pursue this today. He has to deal with paperwork and red tape for three different cases, and it's all shit he can't delegate to someone else. First thing tomorrow, though. That's a different story. He plans to meet the chief of Travis's precinct for coffee at their usual spot. They go way back. Karnaki used to be a cop for this city before he decided he wanted to be an FBI agent more. They have a good rapport.

Slightly sweaty, Karnaki finishes off his day and heads home. It's late, and his wife has probably already eaten, so he stops at a fast food place and orders at the drive thru. He eats on the way home.

There is a limo parked in front of his house, but he doesn't think much of it. His neighbor is a local celebrity, so he figures its for her. He pulls into his driveway and walks up to the front door. It's locked, which is good. He always makes sure his wife knows to lock the door even when she's home. It's a very good neighborhood, but you never know.

"I'm home!" he calls out. First he drops his keys on the table in the foyer. Then he removes his shoes and carefully puts them in the closet. If he doesn't do this, his wife will tear into him. She's a wonderful person, but if you screw with one of her rules, she becomes an animal.

"Ralph! Come on into the living room. You have a guest."

Guest? He isn't expecting anyone. Part of him

wants to draw his gun from under his jacket. He doesn't do it. The neighborhood is, indeed, very nice, and his wife doesn't sound distressed.

"Coming!" He takes his jacket and holster off. Both go into the closet, the latter also going into a gun safe. With that sorted, he turns the corner and enters the living room.

A very pale man with silvery long hair sits in one of the chairs. A walking stick is balanced across his lap, and he is drinking from a tumbler. Scotch on the rocks, probably. He smiles, but somehow it doesn't seem very pleasant.

"Mr. Karnaki," the man says. "My name is Lucifer Robinson, and I would very much like to talk to you. Please. Have a seat." Gesturing to the couch, where his wife now sits.

Karnaki has an odd feeling in his guts. Maybe putting the gun away was a bad idea. Regardless he sits next to his wife and prepares to hear what his visitor has to say.

CHAPTER TEN

Willie Salas keeps an office in a fairly good section of town. The streets are a bit cleaner than usual, and there is only one homeless man sitting in the shelter of a bus stop. He doesn't even bother to panhandle, so Mickey doesn't have to come up with a polite way of saying fuck off.

The building is four stories. It is one of the oldest structures in the city. The lobby is old fashioned, complete with a transom instead of a desk. Mickey nods to the clerk as he walks past. The hunched-over bald man doesn't acknowledge him.

The elevator is so old-timey that there is still a lever from the old days when an attendant operated it. There are buttons on the wall that actually move the car, but Mickey thinks it's a funny kind of thing to leave behind.

When he reaches the top floor, he goes to the door marked with Salas's name, but there is no one sitting behind the desk. From the inch of dust on its surface, it is fair to assume that no one has held the position in a while.

Still, there is perfume in the air. Is Willie with a client? No, the scent is too cheap. More likely a hooker.

Mickey looks at the clock on the wall. A hooker at ten in the morning?

He knocks on the door to the inner office. Something scrambles behind it, and a very low voice can be heard but not deciphered. A click sounds from the desk, and Mickey sees that the intercom is on. "Who is it?"

Mickey steps over to the desk and presses a button on the intercom. "This is Mickey Scarlet. I need to see you about a job."

Click! "Lies. Mickey Scarlet is in prison. Who the fuck are you?!"

Mickey grins and pushes the button again. "Listen, you old bastard. Stop getting your dick sucked for just a second, and let me in."

The cackle is loud enough to hear through the wall. "Come in, Mickey. And watch where you step. I think I got some on the rug."

Mickey pushes through the door, and the first thing he sees is a very large pair of breasts. They jiggle back and forth, nipples aimed at the sky, as their owner wiggled back into her panties. She then struggles a moment to tuck her massive cock back, smoothing out the front.

Behind her stands Willie Salas, zipping his pants up and shrugging into his suspenders. Loose strands of white hair run wildly across his bald pate, and he is grinning so big that Mickey can't help but notice that he isn't wearing his dentures.

"Mickey fuckin' Scarlet." Willie turns his raisin face on Mickey as he pops his teeth into place. "How the fuck are ya? Ain't you supposed to be pounding rocks at the pen?"

Mickey looks at the hooker as she zips her boots up to mid-thigh. "Don't you think it's a bit early for working girls?"

Willie waves a dismissive, liver-spotted hand. "It's a bit late, actually. I haven't slept in days. Goddam cocaine. I think I should come down some. Whiskey?"

Mickey nods and takes a seat across the desk from the PI. Willie takes a bottle of something cheap out of his bottom drawer with two glasses. Just as he finishes pouring the drinks, the hooker holds out her hand.

"What? I fuckin' paid you."

"To fuck." The hooker's English is slightly broken, and it sounds like she had said, "To faaaaahck." There is too much makeup for Mickey to tell her nationality. "You no pay me for cuddle and—"

"All right, all right." Willie scratches his armpits, bare thanks to his yellowed wifebeater. He then hands her a twenty. "You want a job?"

Her eyebrows go up, confused.

"I need a secretary."

The hooker laughs, showing off meth-chipped teeth. Without another word, she slinks out of the room.

"Fuck it," Willie mutters. "I hoped I could get free hummers that way."

"No secretary?" Mickey asks.

"Yeah. It's fuckin' tough, holding on to 'em. You make one comment, and they walk out on ya.

The temp agency won't send me any more girls, and I got about three sexual harassment suits on me. What the fuck, right?"

"I wonder how that happened," Mickey says. He takes a sip of his drink. There is very little quality here, but he has no doubt that it will give him a warm buzz in no time.

"You know, back when I was young a secretary would never even *think* about suing her boss for sexual harassment. It came with the fuckin' territory. Some of 'em even loved the attention. These modern days, I swear."

"How old are you, anyway?"

Willie slugged back his drink. "Who fuckin' knows? I lost track after sixty-five. Anyway, I doubt you came to talk about my fuckin' prostate. What do you need done?"

"Melissa Scarlet," Mickey says. "I don't know if she kept her last name, but just in case her maiden name is Ellis."

"Wife?"

"Yeah. She kind of cut and run on me when I got locked away. I need to get back in touch with her."

"Got a soc on her?"

Mickey, who had done their taxes for years, rattles off her Social Security number. "I don't have a picture of her, though." He does, but he doesn't want to give up one of the few he does. He trusts Willie, but accidents can happen.

"Don't matter." Willie takes a few notes. "I'll find it online. You'd be surprised what the Freedom of Information Act can get ya."

Mickey swallows, and his hands involuntarily wrestle with each other. "She has a kid with her."

"Boy or girl?"

"I . . . I don't know."

Willie looks up from his notebook and notices Mickey's hands. "Shit, Scarlet. I've never seen you like this. You're like a rape victim giving a statement. What gives?"

Mickey forces his hands to come apart, and he reaches for the glass. Whiskey immolates his guts, and his palms stop itching for an axe. "I'm afraid I'll never see her again. I'm scared shitless that I'll never know my kid."

Willie's gruff demeanor melts, and he pours Mickey another drink. "I'm sorry as all hell, son. I'll find 'em both for you. I've never lost a missing persons case. Never."

Willie's sudden shift to a gentle helper throws Mickey off. While the detective probably has never seen Mickey in such a nervous state, the same can be said for Mickey never having seen Willie's lighter side. He almost looks like a kindly old grandfather. It is suddenly hard to imagine this guy shoving a broken bottleneck into a crackhead's face. That had been a long time ago, but still.

"Thanks," Mickey says. "I really appreciate it."

There is a moment of silence before Willie says, "You know my fee."

Mickey can't help but smile at the suddenly broken illusion. "Yeah. Still two hundred a day with a five hundred retainer?"

"Nothing's changed," Willie says. "I'll start today as soon as we fill out some paperwork, all right?"

Mickey nods, finishing off his second drink. His breakfast had been light, and the buzz is already working at dulling his perception. He signs off on everything, and he peels a few hundreds off his wad and hands it over.

Willie cackles in a way that only dirty old men can pull off as he fills out the receipt. "This brings back memories, Mickey. Except this time the cash wasn't passed to me under the table. Good times, my friend. Good times."

Mickey takes the receipt and is about to stand up when a thought occurs to him. "Willie, have you ever heard of a guy named Lucifer Robinson?"

The old man cocks an eyebrow. "Lucifer Robinson? Didn't he used to fight the Shadow or something?"

Mickey chuckles. "No, just a guy I know. I was just wondering if his name had gotten around."

"Jesus. No, I don't think so, but I haven't kept my ear to the ground in a while. The streets haven't talked to me in a long-ass time. You want me to look into it?"

Does he? While Mickey doesn't think his arrangement with Lucifer will ever end well, he does, for the time being, have a good thing going. Why fuck it up? Does the mystery plague him that much?

"Sure. Look into it, but my wife's the priority, okay?"

"Sure thing," Willie says. "I'll give you a call as soon as I got something."

"Thanks." Mickey reaches across the desk to shake the old man's hand, but the detective draws back, grinning.

"You don't want to shake that hand." He sniffs at his fingertips and then licks them. A satisfied sound rumbles in the back of his throat.

"Dirty old man."

"We're all dirty. It's just a matter of how dirty we want you to think we are."

CHAPTER ELEVEN

When the doorbell rings, Mickey thinks it's Lucifer Robinson with a new assignment. He looks at the clock. Eleven at night. Lucifer doesn't strike him as one who is early to bed, early to rise, but he never comes for a visit past six in the evening.

Mickey peers out the window and doesn't see Lucifer's limo. The only odd vehicle out there is something that looks like an unmarked cruiser. It's too nice to be local, though. Fed?

Only one way to find out. He presses the button next to his door. "Who is it?"

"I think you know." The words are slightly slurred. It takes Mickey a moment to decipher it. "Let me up."

The voice *does* sound familiar. Someone he used to work with? He's pretty sure it's a person from his past.

Fuck it. "I don't like guessing games. Who are

you?"

A pause, and Mickey hears the man clear his throat. "It's Ralph Karnaki."

Mickey's teeth throb, and it takes all of his effort to get his clenched jaw to relax. He can't do it. A grinding sound fills his head in a drone, like the humming of bees. His palms sweat, and the beast stirs in his guts. He can feel it slithering up past his heart.

Lucifer had told him that he isn't above the law, that his boss would frown upon spending money to cover up another crime. This implies that Lucifer's superior would regardless do it. Here is his chance to revenge himself upon the man responsible for sending him to jail.

He buzzes the federal agent in.

While Karnaki traverses the stairs, Mickey goes to his bedroom and retrieves his axe. He hasn't had the opportunity to use it yet, but the biggest tree in the forest is now on its way to his door. His hands sing as they grip the handle.

He wants to greet Karnaki at the door with the axe resting on his shoulder, but he doesn't want to play his cards too quickly. Maybe Karnaki wants to come in. Maybe he wants a drink. Maybe . . . maybe while he's sitting down on the very comfortable couch, sipping at a whiskey, maybe Mickey would give him the surprise of his life.

He slips the axe between the chair and coffee table. When he's satisfied that only he can see it, he goes to the door and waits, peering through the peephole.

The beast grows impatient, and its grip slackens. In that moment he realizes that he is planning to commit murder. The beast is not simply satisfied with what he'd done to Arvin Jakowski. It is still bloodthirsty.

That's just the way you are.

Mickey turns and sees his father standing behind him, his head hunched low, the red hole in his forehead dribbling blood. He grins. *There's nothing you can do about it, son. Embrace it.*

Karnaki appears in the convex lens of the peephole, and Mickey twists the knob with a greasy hand. The federal agent stands before him in all of his corpulent splendor. The hair at his temples has thinned and retreated, and the hollows under his eyes are much more pronounced, but it is the same Karnaki as ever.

"Can I come in?" Whiskey breath drifts from his open mouth, and his eyes are so dull it is a wonder he is still conscious.

Yes. Come in. Mickey's father beckons with his thick, meaty fingers.

"No," Mickey says. "State your business."

Karnaki chuckles, but there isn't a trace of humor on his face, not even a slight smile. "I'm not a vampire. It's okay to invite me in."

The beast pokes its scaly head out of Mickey's mouth. "You're worse than a vampire," it says. "You're a fed."

Mickey gags and swallows as hard as he can. The beast slithers back into his mouth and into his guts. Mickey coughs. "You can talk to me right here."

"I'm not here on official business," Karnaki says. "I don't even have a badge on me. I just had to come and see if it was true."

"To see if what was true?"

"Travis told me he'd seen you here the other

day," Karnaki says. "Which is funny because I thought you were stuck in the pen for a few more years."

Mickey's hand aches on the doorknob. He keeps thinking about that axe. "You'll have to go somewhere else for your answers."

"Come on. Let me in for a few minutes. Give me a drink and talk to me. Travis told me about some really strange shit, and the curiosity is just fucking killing me."

Mickey wrenches his hand away from the doorknob, and it curls up into a fist. He fights to keep it hanging by his side. "Fine. Come in, if that's what you really want."

Karnaki steps in, and he looks around the living room. "It's not exactly the best of style, Scarlet, but it's not bad. How much do you have to pay for all of this stuff? Or do you pay?"

Mickey closes the door and considers putting the chain on. It would be one more thing for Karnaki to have to get through if things go south, and the fed tries to run. Still, he doesn't want to make the guy suspicious. He lets it go.

"How about that drink?" Mickey asks.

"Sure. Scotch, if you have it."

Mickey has it. He goes to the kitchen and pours two drinks. When he returns to the living room, he sees Karnaki flipping through the movies and music collection. He seems to have grown fatter in the last couple of minutes. His skin is pinker, and his nose looks more like a snout. His eyes are beady. Piggish.

Karnaki holds a romantic comedy aloft in his hand, which now looks more like a hoof. A laugh squeals out of him. "You watch this shit, Scarlet?"

"Here's your drink." Mickey watches as Karnaki's hoof approaches the drink and somehow encircles the glass.

Karnaki sips at it. "You're not going to answer any of my questions, are you?"

"Have a seat." Mickey gestures to the couch with his own drink.

"No thanks. I'm like a shark when I'm drinking. If I stop moving, I'm dead."

Fine. Make things difficult. Maxwell Scarlet hovers behind Karnaki, a revenant ready for the kill.

Mickey sits in his chair and lets his hand dangle down to the hidden axe. His fingertips brush the soft handgrip, and they start to tingle. He feels it all the way up to his elbow.

"I couldn't believe what Travis had told me," Karnaki says. "Don't worry. He didn't talk until I filled his belly with cheap booze. It took a lot of that shit to get him going, too. You must know someone very, very important."

Mickey waits.

"I checked up on you. Did you know that you don't exist?"

Mickey's heart jumps in his throat, and his fingers retreat from the axe. He never thought he'd be able to get information from Karnaki, but this is definitely news to him. Perhaps Karnaki even knows about Lucifer Robinson.

"Oh no," Karnaki says. "I don't mean the new Mickey Scarlet. I mean the old one. All records of you have been destroyed. Paper files are gone. Computer files have been purged. Mickey Scarlet exists, but he's a different person than the one I put behind bars. So. What gives?"

Mickey looks at him sidelong. "You probably know as much as I do."

Karnaki kills the rest of his drink. "The fuck you say. I've been trying to figure this mess out. I know you exist. I'm talking to you, and you're clearly the same guy I arrested all those years ago. You're not that important, so you must be pulling clout. With whom?"

Mickey grins, showing off his milk-white tombstone teeth. "Maybe I'm a ghost. Ever think about that?"

Karnaki stares at him, and though the fat at his neck is thick, Mickey is still able to see the fed's adam's apple jive and shuck.

"Is this the part where you tell me that you don't know what I've got planned, but you're going to bust me?"

Stop fucking around, son. End him. You won't get another chance. Maxwell playfully runs a finger across Karnaki's throat. Karnaki shivers slightly.

"Well?" Mickey asks.

Karnaki puts the empty glass down on the coffee table, and when he straightens up his eyes are shining. "No. I'm not going to do a goddam thing. Ask me why."

Mickey shrugs. "Why?"

"Because your boy, Lucifer Robinson, paid me a visit. He gave me enough money to send all three of my kids through college." Karnaki laughs, but his tears are so thick he chokes on his own false mirth.

Mickey puts both of his hands into his lap, miles away from the axe. "Welcome to my world, Karnaki. How do you like it so far?"

The fed moves his head back and forth. "I'm not a dirty cop like you. Don't even try to make that comparison."

"If it helps you sleep at night," Mickey says. "Just remember, because you took that money you'll be responsible for everything I do."

Karnaki stands before him, bereft and soulless. "You think I can sleep at night?"

Mickey stands up and gestures to the door. "Great to see you, Ralph. Get the fuck out."

Karnaki stands his ground, wiping the booze sweat from his forehead. Now his hair is wet, and it looks a lot thinner than it had before. Mickey can see crows' feet at his eyes. Karnaki looks aged beyond his years.

"I think you're a ghost, Scarlet. I think maybe you died in prison, and you've managed to find a way to haunt me."

"Shit, Ralph. If that's what you think, I can solve all your problems without an exorcist. Get the fuck out of my apartment and my life, and never come back."

Looking at the back of Karnaki's head as he makes his way to the door tempts Mickey to plant the axe in him anyway. There is something about watching him waddle like a penguin with diarrhea that makes him want to end the fucker then and there.

Just do it, son. Do it before he slips through your fingers.

Mickey ignores his father. Karnaki would have to spend the rest of his life wondering what he could have done to stop the big bad beast.

Just before Mickey closes the door, Karnaki turns to him. "There's one more thing, and then

I'll be out of your life. At least as much as I can be."

"What's that?" Mickey asks.

"Your boy Lucifer might be able to open any door and shut any mouth with his neverending pile of cash, but there are some people in the world who can't be bribed. One of these days such a person is going to put a bullet in your fucking brain, and I kind of hope I'm there for when it happens."

"Just think, you could have been that person. All you had to do is say no to the money."

The fed's lower lip quivers. "I know."

He turns and slithers away into the night.

Mickey closes the door and picks up the axe from its hiding spot. He admires the blade a moment, and he thinks that letting Karnaki go might have been a mistake.

You'll regret it, son. I know you will.

"Fuck off, Dad."

When he looks up, he sees no trace of his father. Good.

CHAPTER TWELVE

The cell phone Lucifer gave him rings. Mickey's face is mostly covered with shaving cream, and he holds a straight razor in one hand. He sets it down and gingerly holds the phone about an inch from his ear. "Hello?"

"Mickey? It's Willie. I need to see you at your earliest convenience."

"You're in luck. There isn't a fucking thing in my planner today. Where and when?"

Mickey memorizes the address and tells Willie that he'll be there in a half an hour. Then he sees that even though he was careful with the phone, the heat coming off his wet face left a wet spot on the touch screen. He wipes it off and rushes through the rest of his whiskers.

Soon he pulls up to a bar. It's only noon, and already Willie wants to whet his whistle. Mickey finds Willie at the bar, eating a cheeseburger and drinking from a giant mug of beer. His fedora hat is on the counter next to him, and his trench coat is piled up on an empty chair. His suspenders are an X on his back. It's one of the things he likes about Willie. The guy is old fashioned. Mostly this is a bad thing, but Willie wears it well.

Mickey takes the bar stool next to the old man. "Afternoon."

Willie swallows a lump of burger and grins, showing off his dingy gray dentures. There are sesame seeds lodged between his falsies, so it looks like his teeth are growing tumors. "You made some good time, kid."

"It sounded important." Mickey pauses to order a glass of whiskey, and the bartender sets it down in front of him. The pour is generous, and the price is cheap. Mickey hands over some money, and he takes a sip of his drink. "What's up, Willie?"

The detective wipes his mouth. "Where you went to high school, was it a classy place?"

"No worse than most. Why?"

"Every high school has a dame that's steaming hot, right? I'm not talking beautiful. I mean outta-yer-league on fire. No one even came close. At my alma mater, it was Mavis Keller. How about yours?"

Mickey considers this a moment. "I guess it would have to be Angela DeForest."

"Ever make her?"

"Very few did. I wasn't one of 'em."

"But you tried, right?"

"Shit, who didn't?"

Willie cackles. "For four years I followed Mavis Keller around like a goddam puppy. I tried every trick in the book, and she fell for none of them. If I'd known which college she was going to, I would have gone there and continued the war. I was practically a stalker. And then a few years later I ran into her at a grocery store. Guess what?"

Mickey waits.

"I tried again, and she finally said yes. We went out a bunch, and she eventually married me. We had a great ten years together before cancer took her. But I will tell you, breaking her was the hardest thing I've ever done. Until now."

Mickey finishes off his drink and gestures for another from the bartender. "Is that what this long, drawn out story was about?"

"I can't find your wife," Willie says. "It's damn near impossible. I've done everything I can think of, and nothing's giving away. It's like someone hid her, and they did a bang up job. Is she in the witness protection program or something?"

"I don't think so. What's the problem?"

"Sometimes I think that she's just disappeared from the face of this earth."

Something about the way Willie says this reminds Mickey of Karnaki's visit. He can't put his finger on it, though. It's enough to send a chill of déjà vu through him.

"But that's not all," Willie continues. "It's more like she's out there somewhere, but any traces she might have left are gone or covered up. I talked with some of my closest buddies on the force, and no one could pull through for me. I just don't fuckin' get it, kid."

Mickey stares into the glass of his replenished drink. He shakes it in a circle and watches the light ice swirl around. Tiny bubbles slither to the top, and his hand gets slick with condensation. "What about Lucifer Robinson? You find anything on him?"

Willie grunts and finishes off his beer. "Yeah, speaking of fucking ghosts . . ." He waves at the bartender and points at the empty, frothy mug.

"Nothing?"

"I didn't say that. Not exactly."

"Then what?"

"The man doesn't exist on paper. Or in any database, or whatever you kids are calling computers these days. But people have clearly *heard* of him."

"What people?"

Willie stuffs a fry into his mouth and chews, contemplating his meal. Mickey is about to repeat the question when the old man looks up. "No one'll cop to it. I talked to some of my contacts on the force, and a couple of them clearly knew who I was talking about when I mentioned his name."

"How high up?" Mickey asks.

"One of 'em's a lieutenant. The other's a captain."

"I was on the force for a long damn time," Mickey says. "Why have I never heard of him?"

Willie shrugs. "These guys, they recognized the name, but when I questioned them further, they kept mum. I talked to some of my street pals, and I got the same result. If I had to guess, these people are a little scared of this guy."

Mickey wonders if maybe he should pay a visit to some of Willie's street contacts. He knows that he could never convince a cop to talk to him but criminals? They would be more inclined, especially if he leans on them a bit. The only way to get people to give up a scary guy is to make yourself scarier than him. He thinks about his axe and wonders how far he would go to satisfy his curiosity.

"If I was a bit younger, I'd slap these punks around and get some answers for you," Willie says. "Time's not been kind to me, kid. But if you want me to pursue this thing, I will."

Mickey downs his drink and leaves a tip on the bar. "That's what I'm paying you for."

Willie grins. "No matter how hairy things get?"

"You're one of the slimiest guys I know," Mickey says. "If anyone's going to find Melissa and figure out who this Lucifer Robinson is, it's definitely you."

Mickey stands and Willie pokes a cigarette in his mouth. "So long, Mickey. I'll be in touch."

Mickey nods and turns away. As he starts his trek to the door, he hears the scratch of a lighter, and before his hand touches the knob, he can hear someone curse. The bartender says, "You can't smoke in here."

"It's okay," Willie says. "I've been comin' in here for thirty years."

"I'm going to have to ask you to leave."

Mickey pauses, waiting.

"I'm gonna have to ask you to go fuck yourself. And get me an ashtray."

"If you don't leave, I'm going to have to call the authorities."

Willie roars with laughter. "Kids today, I fuckin' swear. Back in my day, bartenders had steel in their bones. If you were half the man you think you are, you'd'a belted me in the mouth. Hey Harry! Who the fuck you hiring these days?"

An old man sitting at a table by the door snorts. He is reading a newspaper, and he never moves it from his face. "Young blood, Willie. You know how it is."

Mickey turns around just in time to see Willie grab the bartender by the tie and yank his head down onto the bar. There is a wooden thunk, and the bartender recoils, falling to the floor and out of sight. A mewling sound drifts from below.

Willie peers over the bar. "Quit crying. A broken nose builds character. I should know." He tweaks his own crooked schnoz.

Harry puts down the paper. "Make yourself scarce for a while, willya?"

"Yeah, yeah. I know the drill." Willie drops some cash on the bar and collects his coat and hat.

Mickey smiles. "See? You're not as old as you think you are."

Willie grimaces. "That was nothing. Kicking a dog would've been harder."

CHAPTER THIRTEEN

Another day, another delivery. Heroin again, but the bag is bigger this time. Mickey takes the envelope from Papoulos, and it feels fatter than usual. It noticeably weighs down one end of his jacket. He puts his hands in his pockets to try and compensate.

When Mickey gets home, Lucifer and Lotho are waiting for him in his living room. Lotho sits quietly on the couch, looking blankly at a wall. Lucifer holds his cane under one arm and smiles as he admires a few books Mickey left on the coffee table. Ones he'd purchased himself, not ones he inherited.

"Your taste is interesting, Mr. Scarlet," Lucifer says. "I wouldn't have expected you to spend money on books."

Mickey closes the door. A part of him offended that Lucifer had gained access to his home without his knowledge, but he knows that this isn't *really* his place. It belongs to Lucifer, or whoever pulls his strings. If they showed up in the middle of the night, Mickey thinks that would be a different story.

He makes a mental note to keep his axe next to his bed. Just in case.

"You're not the reading type," Lucifer continues. "In fact, you're not much for any form of entertainment, are you?"

"I read some books in prison," Mickey says. "It stuck with me."

"Ah. Of course. You needed something to occupy your time, didn't you?" Lucifer drops the book he is holding back to the coffee table. "You have something for me."

Mickey nods. He hands over the envelope.

"Good." Lucifer tosses the money to Lotho, who snaps it out of the air like a dog would a treat. The envelope disappears into his jacket pocket.

Mickey sits down in his lounger. "I was wondering if I could ask you for a favor."

Lucifer glances sidelong at him as if he has expected this for quite some time. There is no surprise in the lazy grin under his nose. "We're not in the business of granting favors, but hum a few bars. Maybe I know the tune."

"Melissa," Mickey says. "I want to find her. Can you do this for me?"

Lucifer eases a hand over to the DVD collection. He plucks out a plastic case and opens it up. Light reflects off the disc inside, painting a bright silver spot on his forehead.

"Yes or no?" Mickey's voice has an edge to it. Lotho no longer looks at the wall.

Lucifer holds up a finger, and then he uses it to pop the disc out. He plugs it into the player, and an FBI warning shows up on the TV. Then the menu pops up. It's an old noir film, and it shows a curvy femme fatale and a detective holding a gun. Cigarette smoke makes up the letters of the title.

"That disc didn't have a scratch on it," Lucifer says. "That's a bad sign. It means you don't play it at all, and that's a good movie. You should watch it. These crime books can't be all that stimulates your mind."

"I've never been much for art," Mickey says. "Answer my question before I have to take my aggression out on Lotho."

"Lotho's used to it," Lucifer says. "You can't possibly imagine the beatings I've seen him take. The most important thing, though, is that he keeps getting back up. And he always wins. Sometimes I wonder if he's maybe more than human."

Lotho turns his bullet-dented head toward Mickey. The sunglasses reveal nothing, not even a ghostly peek into the windows of his soul.

"I'm surprised you didn't ask sooner, Mr. Scarlet. Has it been eating at you?"

Mickey stands his ground.

Lucifer sighs. "You're no fun. The answer is, I don't know. I haven't tried. Would you care for me to try?"

Mickey simpers. "Would you? If it's not too much trouble?"

Lucifer slaps his hands together. "I'd love to, Mr. Scarlet! Do you have her Social Security number? It's not the only avenue I can pursue, but it would help."

Mickey recites it. "Aren't you going to write it

down?"

"Eidetic memory." Lucifer taps his temple with a slender finger, and he reads it back to Mickey. "Does this meet your satisfaction?"

Mickey nods.

"Good. Then I'll get back to you on it. In the meantime, you have graduated. Lotho, the papers please."

The chauffer slips a bundle of papers out of his jacket and hands them to Mickey. It is a file folder held together with a rubber band, but it isn't very thick. Inside there are only two papers and a photograph. While it isn't as good as a professional in-studio job, it is an excellently made candid shot of a man drinking from a bottle of beer at a bar. How this guy didn't see the photographer is beyond Mickey.

"Who is he?"

"It's all in the file," Lucifer says.

"You want me to kill him? Is that it?"

Lucifer laughs. "Heavens no! He owes us money. If you kill him, how are we going to get it?"

Mickey nods and looks back at the picture. Greasy dark hair, a layer of stubble on his cheeks, pinkie ring on a fat pinkie finger, a shirt so tight the buttons are barely holding it together around the waist. The beer is cheap. No taste. "How bad you want him roughed up?"

"Nothing permanent," Lucifer says. "Bust a few teeth if you need to, or put his arm in a sling. Whatever you feel is right. But don't do anything to him that he can't come crawling back to us to borrow more money in the future. And if he says he has the money, but not on him, tell him to have it by the following day at noon. If he doesn't have it then, you can start dealing in the realm of the permanent."

"But no killing."

Lucifer's eyes gleam. "No killing."

Mickey thinks about the night with Karnaki, and he knows it's been too long since he'd let the beast out. How long since Jakowski? Two weeks? Three?

When he'd been on the force, the beast came out for a daily walk. If it was penned up for a week back then, it started getting antsy. It started coming out when he didn't want it to.

He hates to think of what it's doing inside of him now.

"When do you want it done?"

"Visit him tomorrow," Lucifer says. "You'll find a list of his hangouts in the file."

"Don't forget about Melissa."

"I'll be in touch."

CHAPTER FOURTEEN

The man in the picture has a name: Bruce Largo. He has a wife, two kids, an apartment on the bad side of town, and a gambling habit. Usually he's able to pay back his loans, but of late he's been dipping into the family savings. It doesn't say in the report, but Mickey can read between the lines. As soon as the savings account plummets, Mrs. Largo takes a tumble down the stairs and has to go to the hospital. The kids back their old man up, but Mickey doesn't need to be there to know what happened when Mrs. Largo called her husband on stealing the kids' college money to blow on craps. The beast roils inside of Mickey. It is eager to meet Bruce.

The guy frequents the back room at several local bars during the day, but it seems that after the usual evening of gambling, he likes to sit out at the bar and get hammered before slithering home to his family. At least, that's what he does when he wins. When he loses he gets a bottle from the liquor store and hides out under the bleachers at the local high school until he has the courage to go home.

Today is Tuesday, which means that Largo is at Yeamon's Bar and Grill on 25th Street. It's the kind of place where you can throw peanut shells on the floor and the stools are still round cushions with four legs on them. The bartender wears his shirt sleeves up at his elbows, and he keeps a fat, ragged cigar—unlit—in the corner of his mouth.

The law had banned smoking inside bars years ago, but the ghostly scent of cigarettes remains. Mickey thinks that nothing short of a wrecking ball can get rid of it, and something tells him the patrons of this place don't mind it all that much.

There are no young people here. All parties are over the age of fifty, and they are clearly regulars, taking up spots at the bar and around the room where they'd spent their evenings for the past few decades. There is no room for new blood here, so Mickey knows he has to be on his guard.

He takes a seat at the bar, and the bartender looks up from cleaning a glass. There is no speech, and the only question in his eyes is, "Who the fuck is this guy?"

"Evening," Mickey says. He orders a drink.

The bartender duly pours it and puts it down on a coaster. "Four bucks."

Easy on the wallet, at least. Mickey drops four singles on the bar and settles in. The tube TV is cracked, but it still receives a good picture of the game. Mickey isn't much for sports, but he doesn't want to seem out of place. He watches while he drinks.

A sudden shout pierces through the wall, and Mickey sees a door behind the bar. Laughter. A few curse words, but nothing else that isn't garbled. The game that really matters in this place.

The bartender grimaces and goes over to the jukebox. He uses his key to get a free song. It's a house favorite, and the regulars sing along, banging their glasses on the bar with the beat. Mickey follows suit.

This is a group of hard drinking men, and Mickey doesn't want to make it seem like he's nursing his whiskey, waiting for something. He belts it back and orders another. It's all right. He can take it.

He's barely buzzed when at midnight the door bangs open, and a group of four guys emerge, counting money and laughing. A cloud of smoke follows them. Mickey thinks Willie Salas would love this place.

One of the laughing men is Bruce Largo. He wears a shirt that has dark patches under the pits, and the buttons are off by one. A single shirttail pokes out of his pants. He carries the rich tang of cheap cologne and even cheaper booze on his body as he slides over to the bar and takes a stool.

"Gimme some Jack, Mac," he says to the bartender. "Make it a double. I just won big."

Mac pours something that looks more like a triple and passes it over to Largo, who pays him with a hundred-dollar bill. The bartender squints at it, holding it up to the light.

"Come on, Mac. You know us. It's good."

Mac runs the marker over it anyway. When it comes up the right color, he gives Largo his change.

Largo leaves three dollars on the bar and guzzles down his drink. "Yes! That hit the fuckin' spot! Gimme another! Hell, give all these people a drink!"

Those who aren't at the bar suddenly crowd Largo, all clamoring for free alcohol. "Jack for everyone!" he calls out.

Mickey keeps out of the crowd. He sips his drink and waits. Soon a shot glass appears in front of him filled with sour mash. He nods his thanks and downs it. He sits around for a while, listening while Largo babbles about his good fortune in the back room. Half of it sounds like bullshit. Then, very quietly, Mickey finishes his drink and leaves a generous tip on the bar.

His car is parked across the street from the bar, and he gets into the driver's seat. He lowers the window slightly, just enough to let some reasonably fresh air in. He's tempted to turn on the radio, but he doesn't want to draw attention to himself. Instead he digs into a newspaper and pretends to read. Every once in a while the bar's door opens, and he looks up to see who it is.

The headlines are grim, as per usual, but Mickey doesn't pay much attention to them. His eyes run almost blindly across the words of each article as he tries to throttle the throat of time.

It's two o'clock in the morning, and he is reading the front page again. This time, he sees movement from the corner of his eye, and he sees someone moving in the alleyway next to Yeamon's. It's Largo, pressing his head against the brick wall to keep him braced up as he urinates into a pile of garbage.

Largo couldn't have left through the front door. Mickey would have seen that. The weasel probably used the back door.

Mickey gets out of the car, but he doesn't close the door all the way. The slamming sound would garner unwanted attention. Sticking to the shadows he glides around the spotlights left by the streetlamps and slips into the alley. His boots are so soundless on the gritty pavement that Largo doesn't hear his approach, not even when Mickey stops directly behind him.

The hissing sound of the stream lessens and then patters against the plastic garbage bags until Largo shakes himself off and stuffs himself away. Mickey waits for the ripping sound of the zipper before he decides to make his move.

"Nice night."

Largo nearly jumps out of his hair. "Jesus! How long've you been standing there?"

He turns, and Mickey sees his eyes are completely white as if covered by cataracts. Largo seems empty. Soulless.

Mickey says, "Fifty grand. Ring a bell?"

Largo gags, and his eyes seem to grow wider, wider. His face isn't big enough for them. "Oh man. Why didn't you fucking say you work for Montenegro?"

Montenegro? A new name. A fresh piece for Mickey's puzzle. Maybe he'll feed it to Willie and see what happens.

"Just give me the money, Bruce. I'd rather keep this pleasant."

Largo's lips wither and draw back, showing off jagged shark's teeth. His nose recedes until it's a mere button with two holes in it. "Maybe you

116

don't work for Montenegro, then. No one pleasant works for that bastard, right?" He laughs an empty laugh and sends a lazy hand up to Mickey's shoulder, pretending to swat him one.

When Largo sees the lack of humor on Mickey's face, he backs up against the piss splattered brick wall. "Shit. I'm sorry. Look, I don't have it on me."

"I was under the impression that you'd won big tonight," Mickey says. "What with all the drink buying and so on."

"I never win *that* big. I only got a couple though. A place like Yeamon's, you can buy the entire bar shots and only be set back, like, thirty bucks or something. You've seen it."

Mickey shakes his head. "I don't think you take me very seriously."

Largo looks Mickey up and down. "Fuckin' hell, man. Look at the size of you. Of course I take you seriously. You work out?"

Mickey shoves a fist into the scumbag's guts and doubles him over. It knocks the wind out of Largo. More than the wind: all the peanuts and pretzels and whiskey he'd consumed that night rushes out of his O of a mouth, where it splatters against Mickey's coat.

Largo stumbles back and slides down the wall into the puddle of his own piss. He holds his belly with one hand and gingerly brushes at his lips with the other. There is a delay in his reaction, as if his brain is five seconds behind reality. Finally, he says, "I'm sorry. I didn't . . ."

Mickey can smell the scumbag's filth rising up from his own clothes, and his hands curl up of their own accord.

"No!" Largo screams. "Please! I didn't mean to!"

Mickey grabs the whelp's feet and yanks him away from the wall so he can more effectively stomp his head. He doesn't know how many times he puts his boot into Largo's face, but he knows that he quickly grows tired of this and switches to battering him around with his fists.

Teeth skitter across the cracked pavement, and blood warms Mickey's knuckles as he bends over the gambler. Even Mickey knows this punishment far outweighs the crime, but he can't stop himself. And it *is* him, not the beast. Where is that bastard? When it comes to violence, it's usually on deck, eagerly waiting to take to the batter's box.

Mickey doesn't even feel its presence.

When Largo stops crying out, Mickey realizes that he doesn't have the stomach for this. He shifts back to his full height and stands, looking down at Largo's crumpled form. He whistles when he breathes, and his grime-streaked hands are trying to cover his face.

"Jeezus," he wheezes. "You didn't have to do that. You fucked me up good. For fifty grand?"

It's a miracle he can even talk. Maybe his blood alcohol content is working hard at keeping him from feeling the pain he will certainly feel tomorrow morning. It's so pathetic that Mickey almost apologizes. How many guys had he beaten the daylights out of? Hundreds? Thousands? He'd never felt guilty about it before. Why now? Why does Largo make him feel differently about it?

Is it the absence of the beast?

His lips form the words, but he knows he will never say sorry. Not to a scumbag who maybe

118

doesn't deserve a beating this severe. "Just have the money by tomorrow. Noon."

"Goddam, you guys are relentless." Largo pokes around in his mouth, wiggling each remaining tooth. "Why don't you call it even? My dental work's probably going to cost me fifty thou."

"If you don't have the money tomorrow," Mickey says, "you won't need to worry about dental work. Be at O'Rourke's Pub by noon. I know you know the place, so don't fuck me around. And don't be late."

Largo moans as another tooth falls out of his mouth. "Yeah. Great. Thanks. Have a fabulous fuckin' day."

As Mickey walks away from the alley, the drying blood constricting the skin on his knuckles, he wonders if maybe he should call the guy a taxi, or at least give him enough cash to get to the hospital.

No. That ain't how it works. Get in your car and leave him be.

Mickey turns to see that his father is walking by his side. His mouth doesn't move when he talks. He grins, and there are maggots between his teeth.

Mickey follows orders. In his old age he finds that he is getting good at this kind of thing.

*

Mickey gets to O'Rourke's at eleven but only to make sure that Largo doesn't get there sooner and set up some kind of trap. The man seems suited toward revenge, especially if done from ambush. There isn't a sign of him in the place, so Mickey takes a seat in a corner booth so he can see both the front and rear doors. The only thing behind him is the wall.

The bartender comes up and asks if he wants something to drink. Mickey orders whiskey and wonders if maybe he's getting to be too much like Willie Salas, drinking this early in the day. He finds that he doesn't care.

He sips at his drink and takes a look around the room. It's classier than Yeamon's by far. The mirror behind the bar is sparkling clean, and the neon beer lights look fresh as if they'd recently been factory delivered. The walls are made of wood paneling, though, and it makes Mickey feel like he's in his father's rec room. There is also a musty odor in the air, not entirely unpleasant but definitely suspect. He can't figure out what it is, but he ceases to care as his nose becomes accustomed to it.

He's on his second drink when the door opens, piercing the dim interior with a bright ray of sunshine. In steps Bruce Largo, and behind him comes a woman and a child, hand in hand.

Mickey looks over to the Budweiser clock on the wall. It's eleven-thirty. Largo doesn't strike him as the kind of guy who is ever punctual much less early.

Largo scopes the room, and when his eyes fall upon Mickey, he turns to the woman and whispers something. Is this supposed to be some kind of ambush? If so, Mickey's not concerned. If the woman is there to call the cops, Lucifer Robinson will just take care of the whole thing.

The woman, clearly Largo's wife, ushers the

child off to a table on the other side of the room as Largo approaches Mickey. When he gets closer Mickey can see his features more clearly. There is tape over the bridge of his nose, and a bandage covers his split brow. His sirloin lips bulge like a male stripper's Speedos, and the teeth behind them are wired into place. Mickey marvels at the sight: the man must have crawled all over that alley, searching out his broken teeth. From what Mickey can see, they're all there.

"Holy shit, Bruce," the bartender says. "What the hell happened to you?"

Largo shakes his head. "Could you just get me a drink?"

"The usual?"

Largo touches his scrambled mouth. "No. Whiskey'd burn too much. I'll just have a beer. The cheaper the better."

"Coming up."

Largo slides into the booth across the table from Mickey. Up close, where the shadows are thin, Mickey can see the bruises more clearly. "Looking good, Bruce."

"Shut the—" Largo stops himself, a pained look on his mangled face. "Please. Be quiet. I have your money."

Mickey feels something prod his knee under the table. He takes the large manila envelope from him and peers into it. A shit load of large bills. He fans his finger over it, and it looks like fifty thousand. Satisfaction. He disappears it into his jacket.

The bartender puts a drink down in front of Largo, who sips at it carefully. He recoils when the beer touches his beet-red lips. "How much you make, workin' for Montenegro?"

Mickey honestly doesn't know how to answer this, so he doesn't. He keeps his poker face on.

Largo grunts. "You're good at your job. If I'd met you sooner, I probably would have quit gambling a long time ago."

"So you've quit now?"

"Shit yeah. I can't live like this the rest of my life. To think how much I've already lost. No wonder my wife thinks I'm a piece of shit."

"The straight and narrow for you, huh?" Mickey asks.

"From now on."

Mickey doubts it. Very few who walk Largo's path are able to turn back. Still he hopes it's the truth. If anything good is to come from this outrageous act of violence, maybe it was worth it to knock this guy's teeth out.

He stands. "Good luck with that."

Mickey pauses at the door and turns around. Largo now sits with his family, and it looks like he is weeping enough tears to choke a rainforest. The woman cradles his head in her slender, delicate fingers while the kid, a little girl, looks away and pretends her daddy isn't crying.

The envelope feels heavy in his jacket. Did Largo raid his kids' college fund to pay off this Montenegro? Or did he go to another loan shark? The latter is more likely, but after a beating like that, would he be so eager to borrow more money?

No, he wants to play it safe. Largo wants to stay away from any potential ass-kickings for a while. It's got to be from his family savings.

Mrs. Largo shhh-es and pets her husband's hair.

Over his shoulder she looks up and locks eyes with Mickey. When is the last time he'd seen such a smoldering gaze? Melissa, maybe?

No. It had been Parker's wife in court.

Mickey watches this scene a moment longer, marveling at it. No matter how much of a fuck-face Largo had been to his family, they still love him unconditionally. How can that be? Are they just stupid?

Mickey wonders how it would feel to be loved like that, and he feels his chest tighten a little.

He passes over the threshold and out into the day.

*

After driving a block, Mickey grabs for his phone and dials Willie. When the old man answers it sounds like he's in a crowded place. An announcer's voice sounds off in the distance, and Mickey figures the detective is at the horse track.

"What's up, kid?"

"You winning anything?" Mickey asks.

"You fuckin' kidding me? I'm here on your case, not to win anything." He pauses, and the crowd roars. "But I do have some money down. Might as well while I'm here, right?"

Mickey laughs. "You find anything out?"

"I don't know yet. I think I might have a visual on an associate of this Robinson guy."

"Big guy, dented head?"

"Nah. Skinny. Pencil mustache. I think he's a fag."

Doesn't sound familiar to Mickey. "The name Montenegro mean anything to you?"

"Jesus, kid. What the hell are you doing? That guy's a serious drug dealer. Mobbed up like a motherfucker. If you're getting mixed up with him, get unmixed. Seriously. Why ask?"

Drug dealer. Makes sense. He thinks about Papoulos. "Never mind. I'll fill you in later." He hangs up.

Later, as he walks up to his apartment, the phone rings. It's Lucifer Robinson. "I hear things went smashingly today."

"You heard right," Mickey says. "When do you want this money?"

"Keep it for the time being. More instructions will follow."

Mickey drops the envelope on the coffee table and settles in with a glass of whiskey and a good crime book. The phone sits next to him, and it remains silent until about eight that evening. Again, it's Lucifer.

"Mr. Scarlet, I need you to deliver that money for me. Are you ready for the address?"

Mickey grabs a pen and paper. "Shoot."

Lucifer recites the information, and about halfway through, Mickey knows whose address it is.

"That can't be. Are you sure you didn't get the addresses switched up or something?"

"I assure you I have not grown addled in my old age."

Mickey's mouth tightens. "Okay. I'll do it now."

"Thank you."

*

An hour later Mickey hands the envelope back to Bruce Largo. The gambler grins, showing off a mouthful of metal. "Thanks. I appreciate it."

Mickey wants to ask him what the fuck he's thinking. He wants to ridicule him. He wants to inquire about his wife's feelings on this loan. A part of him even wants to withhold the money, or to at least warn the careless fool.

He does none of this. Like a good delivery boy, he turns around and walks away.

CHAPTER FIFTEEN

Mickey reads the same sentence for the fifth time before his mind wanders back to the Largos. It seems that he is constantly surrounded by people who don't know how fucking good they have it. Can't Bruce Largo sense the love baking off of his wife? Or is he such a bastard that he senses it and doesn't give a fuck?

Mickey puts the book down open to the page he's trying to read, and he rubs his eyes. Frustrated, he sighs and drops his hands helplessly into his lap.

Something clanks in the other room. Startled, Mickey stands up and looks toward the kitchen door. Someone is shuffling around in there, and he can smell . . . meat cooking?

He steps over the threshold, and it's not his kitchen. It's the kitchen of his old place, and Melissa is at the stove frying up a couple of steaks. A bowl of mashed potatoes gives off a healthy steam, and his mouth waters.

A childish laugh sounds from the living room. Something clashes together. Is it the struggle of two action figures against each other? Or is it a tea cup on a dish at a stuffed animal tea party?

"Melissa," he says.

She starts turning around, but just before he sees her face, the image shifts. She distorts, and suddenly she wears his father's clothing. And then Mickey sees her . . . no, *Maxwell's* face.

Quit your whining. You did this to yourself.

Mickey rushes to the living room, hoping to get at least a fleeting glance at his child, just enough to find out if he has a son or a daughter. He sees nothing, and his heart shrinks into a lump of coal. The room is so empty it crowds him.

He has never felt so lonely in his entire life. It makes him wonder why he's even still here. It would be so much easier to buy a gun and blow his brains out. Is this what his life has come to? Running like a gerbil on a wheel, doing Lucifer Robinson's bidding and drinking himself to death? He'll never find Melissa. Willie's not going to pull through on this one.

Quit feeling sorry for yourself, you sack of shit.

Mickey sinks to the floor and leans against the wall. Sweat seals his shirt to his back. He closes his eyes and feels them burn slightly.

Hands wrap themselves in his collar, and he's pulled roughly to his feet. He opens his eyes and sees his father's face mere inches from his own.

Own your woman. Own your kid. Find 'em and slap some sense into them. They're yours. No one else's.

The thought of hurting either Melissa or his

child makes him queasy. He's torn between wanting to puke his guts out and throwing a punch into his father's jaw. Rage climbs up his throat, and he growls quietly.

Go ahead. You think you can take your old man?

Mickey pushes his father in the chest, and he turns to mist. It takes a moment, but soon the air is clear of all that remains of Maxwell Scarlet. Mickey breathes hard, and he wills his lungs back into some semblance of order.

He sits back down. Picks up the book. Reads the same sentence a sixth time.

And a seventh.

There is a soft knock at his door, but it's so unobtrusive that he thinks it might be a figment of his imagination. He's about to try the sentence an eighth time when it comes again.

Who the fuck can that be? No one has been buzzed in. Lucifer obviously has the outside key, but he usually doesn't let himself in unless Mickey's not home.

It has to be Arvin Jakowski. He's stupid enough to want to try for revenge again. Maybe this time he's standing on the other side of that door with a gun in his hand, ready to fire into Mickey's belly.

He puts the book down, closed this time, and glides softly to the door. It's dim over here, so he doesn't have to worry about anyone seeing his legs under the door or any light being blocked at the peephole. He puts his eye to the glass and sees that it's Arvin's wife Melody. It's not too bright in the hallway, so he can't see much more than her face.

Is it entirely out of the question that she loves

her idiot husband so much she might try to get revenge in his place?

One way to find out. He steels himself and opens the door, halfway expecting to catch a bullet in the guts. Instead he sees Melody Jakowski standing before him, dressed in something she might wear to a fancy restaurant. Her shoulders are bare except for two thin straps, and the V at her front is so far open he can almost see the bottoms of her breasts. Her hair is done up, and a hint of makeup lights her face. The bruises are almost gone, leaving only sickly yellow around her eyes. It's like someone had drawn on her face with a highlighter.

"Mrs. Jakowski?" His lips form the words by themselves, almost like the reverse of the beast.

"Mr. Scarlet, is it?" she asks.

Mickey nods. He can't find his voice.

"I know we haven't really talked a lot, and we probably should have, considering the things that have happened between us."

"I'm sorry about your husband, ma'am. He just pushed one of my buttons, and I couldn't help it."

"Oh no! I didn't mean to give you the impression that I'm here for an apology. No, I'm very glad you did what you did. I don't think I would have had the courage to leave him without your help."

This genuinely surprises Mickey. "He's gone?"

"Yes. I've been thinking about it for years, but I just know he would have found me. I didn't want to look over my shoulder for the rest of my life. Now I know he's gone for good. I just wanted to thank you."

Mickey feels a grimace struggling to rise on his

face, but when confronted with such beauty he doesn't think it will win. "Nobody should thank me for what I did to your husband. That was a bit ugly, even for me."

"It needed to be done, and I thank you for it." She looks behind her and around. Searching? For what? "I know you live here all alone, Mr. Scarlet, and I thought it would be neighborly of me to cook you a meal. How long has it been since you've had some home-cooked food?"

Too long. He thinks of Melissa at the stove with the steak and potatoes. He can almost smell it. It's not just a vision or a hallucination; it's a savory memory.

She puts her arms behind her back, pushing out her breasts. "I . . . uh . . . asked my sister to baby-sit Chris for me. So we'll be alone."

Mickey's eyes linger at her lips, which she is nibbling on, and his gaze drops slowly to her full breasts. He feels suddenly hot. When he looks back up to her face, she has two horns sticking out of her head. Her flesh is a rich red, and her eyes glow yellow.

He can very easily see himself falling into first her arms and then her bed. They can very well live happily ever after together. He tries to imagine himself raising another man's kid, and he's surprised to find it's an idea he's good with. He thinks he can do it right. Chris will grow up to be a very responsible man, and Mickey will grow old with Melody. Maybe they'll move out to the boonies and sit out on their porch at nights, drinking beer and listening to the buzz of insects in a distant field. Maybe they'll fall asleep to the patter of rain on the roof over the porch.

Maybe he'll even live to see grandkids.

All he has to do is forget about Melissa. How hard could that be? She doesn't want him around, and here is a woman who does.

Mickey deflates. His skin crawls as they stand in silence, looking at each other.

Her hands fall back into view, hanging at her sides. Her face is back to normal, and it is slightly pinched. "It's okay. I understand. I'm sorry I bothered you so late." Her words come out slightly clogged.

"No," Mickey says. "I appreciate the offer. It's just that, well, while I do live alone, I'm still married. I love my wife very much." It takes him a moment to realize that he's just lied. While he still loves Melissa more than he has words to express, the divorce had been pretty final.

She waves a hand. "That's okay. I mean, if you want to come over for dinner, that's still fine, you know. I just . . . well, you know."

"It's probably not a good idea," Mickey says. He tries to think of a gentle way to say that he is a very violent man and probably isn't the best choice for her, but as with most things he finds himself searching his cobwebbed mind for words and only finding spiders.

"Well," she says, "goodnight."

"Goodnight." He watches her go into her own apartment before he closes his door. Leaning against the hardwood, he wonders what the fuck he'd been thinking. How long has he spent today in this filthy apartment wondering why he feels so lonely? Melissa is a fool's dream. Why not settle for the beautiful woman next door? The last time he fucked anything aside from his left hand was before prison.

No. Melissa lives in his heart for good. There is no way to exorcise her.

Something moves on the other side of the wall. At first he thinks it might be someone brushing against the plaster, but when he puts his ear against it he hears a very familiar sound. He'd heard it every night when he was a kid trying to go to sleep at night.

Someone is sobbing. The sound is quiet, furtive, but there is definitely someone crying.

He touches the wall and imagines he can feel Melody's warmth as she leans against her side. She stops sobbing, and she makes some kind of shuffling noise. The wall expands slightly, and he can feel her hand pressing through and touching his.

Mickey puts his other hand on the wall, and it sinks in. He feels himself drawn closer, and he presses the front of his body against the wall. Her breasts jut out and into his chest, and he wraps his arms around her. The wall becomes so fluid that it spreads like water, and their lips meet and melt into each other. Their clothes swirl and dissolve until their bodies ooze against into one another. First their hands and knees entwine, and then their torsos, both becoming one body. Their heads occupy the same place, and they can both sense the pleasure running up and down their forms. It is so strong it almost hurts. He almost wants to stop.

He holds her organs in his hands, both inside of her chest. *Their* chest. Their brains touch each other, and he can see her memories. Some are good. These are from before she met Arvin. Some are bad, and almost all of them involve her husband.

Something snaps. She pulls back, and he can sense her fear. Of course. If he can see her memories, she can see his. He wonders what she's seen.

He falls back and hits his head on the floor. It knocks him out cold, and he doesn't dream at all.

*

Mickey opens his eyes and finds himself looking up at the wrong ceiling. This isn't his bedroom. He struggles up to his elbow, and he sees the door. Memories of last night come racing back to him. He moans and wants to pass out again. He doesn't want to think about it.

He stands, and this is when he realizes that he's naked. There is a scaly mess on his belly. It's been a while since he's found that tacky spot down there. He hasn't had a wet dream since high school.

Maybe that's what this is. Nothing had happened last night. Just a dream.

He touches the wall, and it's slightly wet. He shakes his head.

He has the sudden urge to call Willie Salas and see if he's found anything yet. He doesn't do it, though. He knows Willie will call if he finds something, and that's all there is to it.

Mickey's mouth is dry. He needs a drink. A bottle of whiskey crawls across the floor from the kitchen, it's neck dragging its fat body behind it. It nuzzles against his bare foot, and he picks it up. It squeals when he pops the cork, and it is silent as he drinks directly from its guts. He cradles it in his arms like a baby as he takes it with him to the bathroom, to the shower.

INTERLUDE

Karnaki drinks deeply from his glass of scotch and stares at the computer screen. It has Mickey Scarlet's face on it. A mug shot. He also has a few files pulled up in the background. He's been reading and rereading everything he has on the disappearance and/or death of this prisoner. This is all of the information that exists on the old Mickey Scarlet; he has this because he keeps it on his own machine like a memento.

It's eerie. This situation reminds him of a book he'd read back when he was still a local cop. *The Commissar Vanishes*. It describes Stalin's practice of making people disappear not just from reality but also from history. He remembers one spread in particular. Four pictures. They're all the same, except in each successive one someone has been airbrushed out until the final picture, which only shows Stalin.

Who the fuck is this Lucifer Robinson? How

can he make someone disappear like this? It's clear that Mickey Scarlet is still alive, but everything points to a completely different person who just happens to have the same name. But it *is* him. Karnaki saw him in person.

He's not supposed to be doing this. Lucifer gave him so much money it's nearly impossible to launder into his regular income. But it itches at the back of his mind. He just can't let this go. He despises the fact that Mickey would get away with everything. He already got away with killing Parker. So the evidence isn't there. So what? Karnaki knows in his heart that Mickey shot Parker to death. There's too much coincidence, and Karnaki doesn't believe in coincidence.

"Goddammit." He puts the glass down and rubs at his eyes. "Goddammit." Over and over again, under his breath.

"Ralph? Are you all right?"

"I'm fine, Holly. Just . . . working on something."

She walks up behind him and rubs his shoulders. When she sees what's on the screen, she clicks her tongue. "It's always this guy. Why does he bother you so much?"

"He's getting away with murder. I . . . I just can't forget about him."

Holly walks around him so they can look each other in the eyes. "Ralph, you're driving yourself crazy with this. That Robinson fellow did us a huge favor. We're never going to have to worry about not paying bills ever again. So this one guy gets away with murder. He's not the first person to ever do it, and he won't be the last."

"That's no excuse," Karnaki says. "I swore to

up—"

"You made a promise to Mr. Robinson," she says. "If you don't keep that promise, he might take back his money. Or worse. Who knows who he works for? He's probably some mob guy. Do you want to get in trouble with someone like that?"

"It's the principle of the thing."

Holly stares her husband firmly in the eye. "Ralph. Forget it. You're not you when you're looking at this . . . this garbage. You always have bags under your eyes. You mumble in your sleep, and that's when you're not tossing and turning and wide awake. Plus, you're drinking too much."

"Holly. This is a very bad man. I know him, and I know that he'll continue doing horrible things. Can you live with that?"

She turns around and shuts off his computer without closing anything down. She also takes the half-full tumbler from the desk. "Yes. And you'd better learn how to do that, too. I don't like what this is doing to you."

She walks briskly away. He watches her back for a while and sighs. "I don't, either."

He gets another glass of scotch—no rocks this time—and downs three fingers in one go. It's the only way he knows how to get to sleep these days. Sobriety will keep him up all night. He wonders if Travis feels this way, too. Or the police chief. Or anyone else Lucifer has bribed.

Can Karnaki be the only one who does?

CHAPTER SIXTEEN

Lucifer isn't even halfway up the stairs when Mickey opens the door so fast and hard it crashes into the wall. "Did you find her?"

Lucifer slows his pace, and Lotho nearly runs into him. Lucifer doesn't notice. "Eager?"

Mickey's palm starts to cry, and he forces himself to unfurl his hands. Thin red crescents dribble around his heart line.

Lucifer plugs a cigarette into a holder and gently touches a flame to the end. "Let me in, and we'll discuss it."

Mickey is half tempted to yank the cigarette out of Lucifer's face and stomp it. He doesn't, though. He knows that Lucifer might actually have information for him. Judging from the playful demeanor, he has to have something.

The cigarette stays where it is, and Lucifer slithers across the threshold.

Inside Lucifer takes his customary spot on the

couch and leans his delicate chin on the head of his cane, casting his gaze about the room. Mickey doesn't know why he does this. Nothing ever changes here, so there's nothing new to take in.

Lotho leans his beefy frame against the wall and towers over everything except a halogen lamp. He blocks its light, veiling his features in shadow.

"Well?" Mickey asks.

Lucifer slips a hand into his suit coat and pulls out his flask. He takes his time in unscrewing the top, and when he drinks, he drinks deeply.

Mickey wants to cut through the bullshit, but he figures any interruption at this point will only prolong the suspense. He waits, arms crossed in front of his chest.

When the flask is back in its place, Lucifer sighs through a smile. "We have a new job for you. It's a bit more interesting this time around, since we want you to dis—"

"I don't want to hear about it," Mickey says. "Melissa. Progress?"

"No."

The answer comes without hesitation, and it feels like a knife being jabbed into his throat. All that build up for nothing? Lotho or no, he wants to grab Lucifer by his skinny throat and throttle real answers out of him. Something crowds up inside his upper chest. The beast is stirring.

"I haven't found a single thing," Lucifer says, "and it wasn't from lack of trying, believe me. Someone wants her hidden, Mr. Scarlet, and they want her hidden very badly. Perhaps you should talk with your old friend, Ralph Karnaki. I think he might have snuck her into a witness protection program."

"No way," Mickey says. "Why would they do that? I was supposed to be in prison a lot longer than I was. What would have made her paranoid enough to want to go into hiding? She's out there somewhere, and you've got to find her."

"Calm down. We're still working on it. I've already pulled in several favors for this. In the meantime I'd like to discuss the next thing you're going to do for me."

Mickey is reluctant to let the Melissa conversation go, but already the beast is dissipating. What's the point? The man said he was trying and coming up with nothing. Just like Willie Salas.

Unless, of course, Lucifer is lying. Mickey is very good at figuring out who is trying to spin a fetid brown web of bullshit, but with Lucifer he's uncertain. He gets the impression that this guy lied so much that he transcends the very idea of bullshit.

Lotho hands over a packet of papers. Inside are the usual documents and a picture. It's another gambler, but this one is far too skinny to be a regular winner. In fact, he has a bit of a meth-gaze in his eyes, and Mickey wonders if maybe the fucker is a junkie.

He doesn't have to wonder for long. The report betrays his addiction to heroin and his habit of borrowing money he knows he can't pay back. He stole his own wife's jewelry and even his own kid's toys for some quick cash. A real scumbag.

"Same as before?" Mickey asks.

"No. Ben Fulton is a junkie, and junkies are never good with their money. This is to send a message that we are not to be trifled with."

"No killing," Mickey says.

"I've said it before, haven't I? You don't have to kill him. But I want him beaten within an inch of his life. Break lots of bones."

"It shouldn't be that hard. He doesn't look like much."

"I want you to get a baseball bat," Lucifer says, "and meet him at the location I mentioned in the report. I want you to break his legs and arms and to stomp on his balls. This is all about sending a message, you understand."

"And if he offers me the money?" Mickey asks.

"Not interested. Take it if you want, but don't forget to beat the ever-loving shit out of him."

"Okay," Mickey says. "There's just one more thing."

Lucifer waits, grinning.

"Are you lying to me about Melissa?"

Lucifer doesn't even twitch. "No, I'm not. We're doing the best we can to find her."

Mickey waits for his bullshit detector to go off, but it remains silent in his head. After a moment he nods. "Okay. Thank you."

Lucifer gets up to leave, and he gets as far as the door when Mickey clears his throat. "Do I work for Montenegro?"

Lucifer smiles when he hears the name, and Mickey thinks that is the closest the pallid man ever comes to being surprised. "You have on several occasions," he says, "but you are not in his employ. You were merely out on loan."

"And I'm working for him this time?"

Lucifer nods. "Why? Any moral objection?"

Mickey considers this for a moment. As far as

he can tell Montenegro is a sleazy drug dealer, but how different is he from Mickey himself? While he was on the force he did nothing different.

Lucifer chuckles. "I didn't think so." He glides out the door and down the stairs with his lumbering giant behind him.

Mickey closes the door and grabs a bottle of whiskey. At least he has learned something. It isn't much, but now he knows a little bit about his situation. It's not enough, though, and he's sure it never will be.

*

The next afternoon he goes to a sporting good place and examines the baseball bats on the rack. Most of them are aluminum, and he can't help but think they wouldn't be very good for his purposes. It's just something about them. Maybe it's because he'd always had wooden bats when he was a kid and thought he was going to be a major league player someday. The crack of a line drive just doesn't sound the same on a metal bat as it does on a wooden one.

He takes down a Louisville Slugger and tests the grip, wondering if maybe he should put some tape on the handle. The club seems to be the right weight, and it isn't so thick that he wouldn't be able to hide it.

"Can I help you, sir?"

Mickey looks over his shoulder and sees a man dressed up like a referee, cap and all. "No thanks," he says. "Just browsing."

The salesman doesn't get the hint. "So you, uh, play in a local league?"

Mickey takes a practice swing. "I guess you could say that."

"My son, he plays for the Rockets. They're a local team. Where do you play?"

Mickey glances at him, giving him the hardest eyes he can. He used to do this when he was a cop and wanted to scare the mortal shit out of a scumbag. This also worked well in prison.

The salesman flinches. "Well, if you need anything, please let me know."

Mickey nods and turns his attention back to the bat. He senses the salesman making his escape and is satisfied. The handle does need some tape after all. He would see to that right away.

*

As Mickey approaches the neighborhood mentioned in Lucifer's file, he becomes slightly suspicious. The streets are too clean, almost good enough for the tourists. This isn't the kind of place you're likely to find a junkie.

He finds the property across from 1598 S. Benson Avenue and is surprised to find that it's a park. Not just a place where you can walk your dog, but there is also a playground for kids.

He doesn't think he'll look at home in a park, so he stands across the street and scans people's faces, trying to find the one that matched the picture in Lucifer's folder.

There he is. It's hard to be sure at first because he's lying down on his back, propping his head up with his spindly elbows on the grass. He is slightly turned to the side, and all he can really see is the guy's hair and absurdly large nose.

Next to him sits a young woman dressed in a tight t-shirt and even tighter jeans. They are clearly in love, considering how closely they're talking and how they touch each other at various times. Neither of them wear wedding rings, so Mickey figures this isn't Fulton's wife. This is his *side action*. They both watch the playground with every other glance. He doubts Fulton is here with his own kid, so they're probably keeping an eye out for hers. Or maybe Fulton's the father. There are too many variables to be certain.

Does Lucifer expect him to break this junkie down in front of this girl and her kid? It makes no sense. No one does that kind of thing. Do they? Well, maybe the Russians. They're kind of fucked in the head. But no one else would.

Mickey ducks into a nearby alley and slips the bat out from under his jacket. It takes him a moment to find a good hiding place: just behind a storm drain, where it is barely out of sight yet very easy to reach.

He crosses the street and walks across the grass toward the junkie. When he's sure he's gotten the guy's attention, Mickey pauses stiffly and makes a face as if he's just smelled the inside of a garbage truck on a hot summer day.

"You okay, mister?" the woman asks.

Mickey examines the bottom of his shoe. All he sees are some rogue strands of grass clipping stuck in the treads. "Dammit. I just stepped in dog shit."

The junkie laughs. "You gotta keep your eyes open around here. Owners don't pick up after their fuckin' dogs. It sucks."

Mickey makes as if he's scraping the mess off

his shoe by shuffling his feet in the grass. He then steps closer to the junkie. "You wouldn't happen to be Ben Fulton, would you?"

The junkie squints up into the sun to examine Mickey's face. "That's me. I know you?"

"You mean, you don't remember me?" Mickey offers his best smile. "I'm Paulie Stevenson. We met at Montenegro's place a couple of years ago."

"Oh." The realization comes across Fulton's face so strongly it might as well be tattooed on his forehead and cheeks.

"We had some good times," Mickey says. "About twenty grand worth, as I recall."

Fulton nods. "Yeah."

"You know, Montenegro's kind of pissed that you never got him back. He told me that if I should ever see you, I should mention the money."

"I don't have it," Fulton says. "Sorry."

"He figured you wouldn't. Say, you want to get a drink for old time's sake? Since I'm over here, anyway?"

Fulton looks at his woman, who is watching the playground. He then looks back at Mickey, his eyebrows raised up in a plea.

Mickey shakes his head.

Fulton says, "Honey, why don't you get Matt and go on home. I'm going to catch up with my old friend here."

"Are you sure?" She looks up at Mickey, shielding her eyes from the sun with the flat of her hand.

"I'm sure. Go on, it's okay. I'll see you later."

He looks back up to Mickey as if to ask, "I can see her later, right?"

Mickey nods. "Come on, Ben. Let's get that drink and catch up."

Fulton stands and wipes grass and dew off his palms using his jeans. "Love you, honey." He bends down long enough to peck at her lips.

As soon as they're out of earshot, Fulton trembles slightly. "That was a shitty thing to do."

"You want that woman and her kid to see this?" Mickey asks.

"It's my kid, too. And it's still a shitty thing to do. What's your real name? And don't say Paulie whatshisname."

Why not tell him? "I'm Mickey."

"Great. I'm gonna get the shit kicked out of me by a guy named Mickey. Makes me feel like I'm in the moving pictures. Where are we going?"

Mickey points out the alley.

"Sure. That looks like a great place to get my spleen twisted."

"You shouldn't have borrowed money you knew you couldn't pay off," Mickey says.

"And what? Let my family starve? Do you have any idea what this economy's like? It's not as if I can get a MasterCard. My credit rating's in the toilet."

Mickey doesn't need the beast to take this guy down. He wants to do it himself as soon as possible. "Don't give me that shit. You spent it all on heroin."

Fulton sighs. "Fuck it. All right, so what? Don't you judge me. I'm sure you're fuckin' flawless, am I right?"

"Just get in the alley." It would be a pleasure to break this whiner's bones.

The junkie walks in about ten feet. "Say when."

He continues walking as if he doesn't have a care in the world. How many people are that willing to dive into a merciless beating? It throws Mickey off his game, and when he thinks about it later, he'll wish he'd been a bit more vigilant.

Mickey reaches for his bat behind the storm drain. "When."

Fulton whirls on him. His skin is covered with lizard scales, and his snarling mouth shows off teeth made of heroin needles. His right hand is now a small pistol, and it cracks. Mickey involuntarily shrinks back, trying to make the smallest target possible. Chips of brick from the wall rain down on his cheek. He'll have a bruise later on, but right now he barely feels it.

Mickey falls away from himself, and hair bristles out of him all over his body. His senses are preternatural, and he can feel fangs in his own mouth. He's no longer in the driver's seat. He can see through the twin holes that are his eyes. It's like watching two big movie screens.

The beast is on the junkie in two seconds. Fulton tries to fire again, but the thing that had been Mickey Scarlet mere seconds ago is standing right in front of him as if he'd teleported himself there. Mickey swings the bat—no, now it has shifted into a giant femur bone—and it pulverizes the junkie's gun. It falls off his wrist and rattles away down the alley.

Fulton tries to scream, but there is no time. The femur comes down again, this time destroying his one good hand, which is now cradling its injured brother. Fulton falls to his knees, breath stuck in his throat, eyes wide.

His head is in the strike zone, so the beast

swings the femur again. It connects solidly with Fulton's mouth, and the heroin needles splinter and clatter on the pavement. He falls back, and his head is surrounded by a halo of broken needles.

It's not enough for the beast. It brings the femur down again and again on Fulton's ankles. His bones are sticking out of the flesh, and the beast continues to turn them into paste.

The beast is not mindless. It remembers that Lucifer wants Fulton's balls stomped. It brings its large, shaggy claw down between the junkie's legs so hard it can almost feel the coccyx through the skin. It hears two pops and knows that Fulton will never sire another child.

The beast pants from the exertion of this beating. Its arms are tired from breaking the junkie to pieces. It wanes, and the hair disappears. The fangs recede. Mickey feels himself engulfed by the movie screens, and he's back in control of himself. Fatigued, he lets his blood splattered hands fall to his sides. Not enough to drop the bat, just in case the junkie had some surprise juice in him. But he knows the job is done.

Fulton's arms and legs are twisted at horrible, unnatural angles, and Mickey wonders if the scumbag will ever walk again. Two of the fingers on his left hand are curlie-cued like a pig's tail.

He prods Fulton's chest, and something rattles inside his body: the junkie's breath. Still alive.

"Stupid bastard," Mickey mutters. He bends to scoop up the gun. It isn't much, just a .22, but it might come in handy. He slips it into one of his pockets and gives the junkie one last look.

Steady breath. He's not going to be happy when he wakes up, but he'll be alive. And hey, if he makes it to the hospital, they'll be sure to give him some good drugs. Maybe he should be optimistic about this.

Mickey thinks about calling 911, but why bother? One side of the alleyway belongs to a restaurant, and there's a dumpster back here. Eventually someone is going to come out to throw something away, and they'll find him. That's good enough for Mickey.

He notices that there's some ugly blood splatters across his pants and shirt. Nothing he can do about it. He's got a coat in the car, and he's pretty sure it will cover up the mess. He makes sure no one is watching him, and then he casually walks to his vehicle. No one notices, and no one cares.

On the drive home, he feels his cell phone vibrate, but he doesn't answer. If he gets pulled over for talking on a phone while driving, the cop will definitely see the blood stains. Lucifer might not be able to get him out of a jam that serious.

He parks in front of his apartment and reaches into his pocket. There's a voicemail message, and when he retrieves it, he hears it's from Willie Salas.

"I need to talk with you, Mickey. Something's come up, and I think you should know about it. I'm on my way over to your place right now."

Mickey hangs up. It sounds important, and if it's about Melissa he wants to know right away. He puts his coat on and holds it shut. By now the blood has dried on his pants, so it doesn't look too bad.

Inside he grabs two glasses and a bottle of whiskey. He puts it all on the coffee table, pours himself a drink and waits for the old bastard to show up. He vibrates so hard it seems possible for him to rip through his own skin.

But he waits. And waits. And waits.

CHAPTER SEVENTEEN

Mickey opens his eyes, feeling slightly drowsy. He yawns, and when he looks at the clock on the wall, he realizes that he'd passed out for three hours. What the fuck? He checks his phone, but there are no calls or messages from Willie. It can't possibly take him this long to get here. Mickey wonders if maybe a hooker might have waylaid Willie, but no. He sounded too frantic on the phone.

Mickey stands and goes to the window. He scans the street hoping to see Willie's old Caddy out there. Nope. Nothing. Just the usual collection of junk mobiles.

Something must have happened to him. Mickey tries calling him, but the phone doesn't even ring. It goes straight to voicemail. He doesn't bother to leave a message.

There is no booze left in the bottle he'd brought out to share with Willie. Mickey doesn't remember drinking it all, but it's certainly possible that he doesn't remember doing it. He walks to the kitchen, and when he flicks on the light he sees an odd object on his table.

A hat.

A fedora.

Mickey picks it up by the brim and gives it a cursory glance. The band is a bit ratty, and the top is creased too deeply from many years of use. The scent of sweat and cologne comes off the inside. Old Spice.

Willie's brand.

The label on the inside can't be seen through the thin sheen of coagulating blood. The hair on Mickey's neck starts tingling, and he turns around, facing the fragment of the living room that he can see.

"Willie?" he calls out. "Are you here?"

Mickey heads to the couch and bends down to look under it. It's the only place in this room where Willie can hide. There isn't a lot of space down there, but Willie's a short, skinny guy.

Nothing but dust bunnies.

He checks the front closet, the shower, the bedroom, everywhere. No Willie. He tries calling Willie again. Once more, it goes straight to voicemail.

"Fuck."

Sweat drips into his eyes. He doesn't know what to do, and it's getting hard for him to breathe. Had Willie actually called him? Of course he had. His call is still on Mickey's cell phone. He clearly has information Mickey needs, that Mickey might not get now. Where the fuck is that old man? Sure, he's old, but he's a tough son of a bitch. The toughest bastard Mickey knows. Willie is more than capable of taking care of himself.

Mickey thumbs a damp spot just above his brow, and when sweat comes back to fill it in again, he rams the back of his hand into it. The bristles of his arm hair scrape audibly against his skin.

He's in the bathroom, washing his face, when the television in the living room suddenly turns on. He pauses, looking into his own reflection. His skin crawls. He feels like a person who has just seen a ghost. He quickly dries off his face and walks toward the living room. He wishes he hadn't left the baseball bat in the car.

Mickey looks at the television, and it is completely white with an odd amorphous shape in the middle. It slowly comes into focus, and he recognizes it for what it is: Willie Salas's decapitated head.

It winks at him. "Sorry, kid. They got me. You're gonna have to do this on your own."

"Willie? What happened?"

"Can't stay and chat. Don't worry too much about it. I have it on good authority that you're gonna find your woman and your kid. By the way, you have a—"

The image cuts out. The TV turns off, as if someone doesn't want Mickey to know what he has.

Mickey roars and rushes to the bedroom, to where he keeps the axe. As soon as he touches the handle, reality blurs. It distorts into fast-motion waves. He doesn't remember what happens next. He has a vague recollection of the sound of his boots clomping down the stairs, but he can recall nothing more.

He comes back to himself in his bathroom, washing wood chips and splinters out of his hands. A red spot on the web between his index finger and thumb sang as he rubbed soap into it. It's already turning into a pale, tumor-like blister.

He dries his hands as he goes to the front window. He doesn't know what he's done, but he knows it happened outside. Surveying the world, he tries to see what is different about the neighborhood. He locks onto a skinny maple tree, far from adulthood, lying on the street. Its stump is a stake pointing at the sky, waiting for a vampire to fall on it.

Did anyone see him doing this?

He surprises himself by not even caring.

Mickey brings the axe back to its place by his bed, and he goes back to the kitchen for another bottle of whiskey. He drinks directly from its neck. Fire kindles his guts as if he is a stove, and he slumps down into a chair.

Willie's hat is still on the table, so Mickey picks it up and examines it. Can it really be true? Is Willie Salas really dead? Mickey can't envision a world without Willie in it.

The door buzzes. Mickey goes to the intercom and presses a button. "Who is it?"

"Police, sir. Please let me in. I have to ask you questions about an, uh, incident."

Fuck. Mickey sighs and buzzes the cop in. He opens the door and waits to see if it will be a familiar face. It turns out to be some kid, probably fresh from the academy. No one from Mickey's past.

"Are you Mickey Scarlet?" he asks.

"I am."

"My name is Officer Michaels. Sorry about this, Mr. Scarlet, but the captain wants me to put on a good show for the neighbors."

"What do you mean?" Although Mickey is pretty sure he knows.

"Well, thanks to your benefactor we can't really do anything to you for this. But we can't have the public wondering about it. Once they start to think about things, it usually leads to corruption charges. No one wants that right now. It's an election year."

Mickey grunts a short laugh. "I see. And do you know Lucifer Robinson personally?"

"Oh no," Michaels says. "My boss does, I think. I just know I'm supposed to give you a visit and leave your neighbors with the impression that I gave you a ticket. I'm getting a decent bonus for this, as I'm sure you can guess."

Michaels is just a font of information. Mickey wonders if this rookie even knows what he's doing is illegal. He seems too fresh-faced and innocent.

"Consider your impression given. Care for a drink before you go back out there?"

"No sir. Never on duty."

Mickey almost laughs. He should have known better.

The candlestick phone rings for the first time in ages. The prankster. He's the only one who ever calls that number. His soul numb, Mickey picks up the ear piece and waits.

Laughter, same as always. "Fuck you, Mickey Scarlet."

Mickey doesn't say anything.

"You hear me, you cocksucker? Fuck you. Fuck you. Fu—"

Mickey hangs up. He just doesn't care.

*

The next morning Lucifer stops by with Lotho in tow. They waltz in as if nothing is different about today.

"You did so well with your previous job that we have another one for you," Lucifer says. "Have you ever—?"

"Willie Salas," Mickey says.

"Pardon me?"

"Have you ever heard of a private investigator by the name of Willie Salas? William Salas?"

Lotho clears his throat into a hand the size of a bowling ball, but he says nothing.

Lucifer puts a finger to the cleft of his chin and taps twice. "Why does that name sound familiar?"

Mickey hands Lucifer the bloody fedora. "I think you know him."

Lucifer examines the hat and turns it over in his hands a couple of times. "You know, I think you're right. Didn't I see something about him on the news this morning?"

Mickey stares at him, not trusting himself to speak or even move.

"I did," Lucifer continues. "I heard he'd been dismembered. Very ugly business. Why can't the mob stick to the classics, like shooting your enemy in the head and heart? Now *that's* a way to go out."

Mickey nods, but not because he agrees with

156

Lucifer. No, Mickey thinks about classics and about how old fashioned Willie had been.

"What about him?" Lucifer asks.

"He was a friend, and I was hoping there was something you might know about what happened to him."

"My superiors may be powerful, but omniscience is sadly not in their oeuvre, I'm afraid."

"Shit," Mickey says. "I was hoping you could find the son of a bitch and get some revenge for the old man." He waits, watching Lucifer's face.

Nothing changes. The bastard is as calm as ever. Why does he have to be so hard to gauge?

"Well, I wish you luck in this endeavor," Lucifer says. "In the meantime we have another job for you. Lotho?"

The giant hands over a new packet, and Mickey leafs through it.

"I hope you still have that baseball bat," Lucifer says.

Mickey glances at him over the top of the file. He grins, but there is nothing friendly about it. It looks like the last thing a bird would see before a cat's teeth close around it.

CHAPTER EIGHTEEN

As Mickey pounds some junkie's kneecaps to powder, he considers hiring another private investigator. It's an idle thought, and he doesn't put much weight behind it. If Lucifer Robinson can find out about Willie Salas and kill him, why wouldn't he do the same thing to another detective? Besides, Willie was the only one who could have done it. If something's shady in this city, Willie knew about it. He may have been a dirty old man, but he knew his shit.

No, Mickey is going to have to do this himself.

The junkie is beyond gasping. His eyes roll back into his head, and he jitters like a massage bed in a cheap motel. Who is this guy, anyway? Mickey remembers reading the file, but he's damned if he can recall any of the info he'd gone over. These dickheads are blurring together. Not that it matters. The message has been delivered, and it is time to go.

He reaches the end of the alley before he turns around to see the guy on his back, scrabbling at the loose pavement with his ragged fingernails. One foot kicks up and down, and his back arches to the beat.

Is this guy faking it?

Shit. Mickey goes back to the junkie, keeping one hand up to guard his face should this be a trick, and he bends down for a closer look. Saliva pools in the corners of the junkie's mouth, and it bubbles a little. His eyes are so far back they're pure white. Is he choking on blood? Or is this some kind of seizure?

Mickey considers calling 911, but by the time an ambulance shows up, the junkie will be dead. Having no other alternative, he stomps the junkie's guts. A whooshing sound flies out of his mouth, and he hacks up mucous. It is tinted red.

At first relief passes across the junkie's face like a gentle ocean wave, and then he starts crying as the pain sets back in.

Satisfied, Mickey walks away back to the street where his car waits for him. He drops the baseball bat in the trunk and drives to the nearest burger place. He dines in, thinking that Willie Salas had liked this restaurant. It's just sleazy and grimy enough for his likes.

Now he doesn't like anything. Mickey grimaces at the thought and the realization that if he hadn't hired Willie, Willie would be alive right now.

Mickey thinks about resigning from the apartment, from the constant stream of money, from the violent jobs, from everything, but he knows that if he does he would never see Lucifer

Robinson again, and he needs that pale fuck as close as possible if he's going to find Melissa.

Mickey finishes his food and drives back to his apartment. On the way he calls Lucifer and tells him the deed has been done. Later he barely remembers the conversation. His routine is getting so familiar he can probably do it with both eyes burned out of his skull.

At home he sits in his chair and sips his whiskey while staring at the blank TV screen. He can still count the number of times he has used the television on the fingers of one hand, and he doesn't feel like reading.

Finding Melissa is the one thing that keeps banging around his frontal lobe. If someone as smart and resourceful as Willie Salas couldn't do it, then what hope does Mickey have? Except the old man had said that he had something. It has to be about Melissa. But what if it's about Lucifer or Montenegro instead?

This task would be much easier if Melissa has friends or family or . . .

Well, she *does* have friends. Her college roommate lives in Ohio. Her best friend since high school is in Kansas. Doesn't she have an aunt in Pennsylvania?

But he doesn't remember their names, much less their contact information. How the hell can he find them?

It's an hour before he turns his thinking to his old house in the boonies. Melissa had sold it shortly after he was sentenced, but who had bought it? Would the owner allow him to check it out, maybe search for an overlooked clue that didn't move on with Melissa?

He finishes off what is left in his glass and grabs his keys. It's only eight o'clock, and the sun is still up, even though it's only a faint smudge on the horizon. He doesn't consider the whiskey on his breath, but he knows he's on a roll. No one can stop him now.

*

The sky is a gaudy shroud over the city by the time he makes it out to his old house, and the clock says it's nearing nine. Traffic at this hour is easy, although it takes him several times to get the correct gravel road. Has it really been that long since the last time he'd been here?

As he draws nearer to his old property he sees the house as a shadow silhouetted against the cobalt sky, where there is just a faint shimmer of sunlight left like the final ember in a campfire at dawn.

There are no lights on in the place, and there are no vehicles in the driveway.

By the time he parks his car, he knows that no one lives here. Everything seems too hollow, too bereft, to be a suitable domicile.

As he goes up the creaking, spider-webbed steps he sees a porch swing swaying in the breeze. A shadow sits in it, drinking what looks like whiskey and watching something on the lawn. Mickey turns to see a crackling figure. A child. Sometimes it's a little boy, and sometimes it's a little girl. The kid is playing.

When he looks back at the swing he sees that the figure is now watching him. Mickey steps forward just in time to see that the stranger wears his own face. This apparition winks at him and fades away. The child is gone, too.

There is also a rocking chair on the rickety porch, but it looks so old and weatherworn that it would probably snap into splinters if he tries sitting on it. Not that he isn't tempted.

The door is locked, but the wood is so far gone he doesn't need to do more than jiggle the knob before it pops open.

Inside the place has a musty odor like an old neglected attic. There are webs everywhere and mouse droppings sprinkle the floor like confetti. Some of the furniture is still here, covered in sheets.

Mickey rolls the covering away from his old chair, the one he used to sit in while relaxing in front of the fireplace. It still looks new. Nothing dirty about it. He sits down and sinks in, dust poofing out from under him. It's still as comfortable as he remembers.

The fireplace yawns in front of him, and he considers chopping down a tree just to get some wood for a fire. It sounds like a lot of work, and besides it's a bit too dark out right now. No, he'll settle for this.

He pulls out a pint of bourbon that he'd bought on the way over. It warms his belly and makes him nearly pleasant enough to travel back in time to when this chair was truly a comfort.

He stares into the fireplace as intently as if it is a crystal ball, but he gets nothing out of it. How many schemes had he conceived of while sitting in this very spot? Schemes that would eventually put him in prison. Schemes that lead up to this moment. Full circle? No. To come full circle he needs to have some form of satisfaction, and that is one emotion he hasn't felt in a long time.

It takes him another hour to pull himself up far enough to start looking around. None of the lights work, so he goes back to his car for a flashlight.

When he gets back inside he goes over every damned inch of the house. It's hard work not because it's dark or because there are a lot of places to check, but because he has to stop every once in a while. Melissa is in their old bed, the one where they'd made love for the first time as a married couple. The bed sheets barely cover her curvy frame, and she waves to him, smiling through a veil of messy hair. He almost gets into bed with her, but she fades away, leaving only the faint scent of her flowery perfume.

He finds himself in the kitchen. He's wearing his old street cop blues. Melissa is there, too, and she's cooking what smells like steak. Mickey remembers this as the day he got promoted to plainclothes. He steps up behind her, intending to put his arms around her, but when the other version of him tells her the good news, she turns around, a grin on her face, and rushes at him. Mickey feels her pass through him like a ghost, and when he turns, he sees them embracing. Melissa pecks kisses all over the past version of himself.

Mickey's eyes burn a little, and he can't bear to watch them. He can't bring himself to look away, either.

They fade away. Mickey sniffs at the air, searching out the smell of cooking meat. Nothing.

He finds them again in the bathroom. The past version of Mickey leans on the sink, tapping his foot. Melissa sits on the closed lid of the toilet. He doesn't need to see her hands to know what she's holding. He remembers all too much the day she took the home pregnancy test.

Mickey can't see this again. It will break him. He closes the bathroom door and puts his back to it, sinking to the floor. This time the tears flow freely. He doesn't sob. He doesn't think he'll ever be able to sob again. He waits. Waits. Waits.

The scene has to be over. He wipes his eyes and opens the door. A part of him almost hopes that they're still there, making love against the wall in celebration.

They're not.

It's near midnight when he decides there are no clues here. He wonders if Willie has been here, but in his search he finds no sign of the old man. The whole fucking thing is hopeless.

Mickey goes back downstairs and collapses into the chair. It's time to finish off this pint, and he does it quickly. Maybe too quickly, because when he tries standing to go home, the room tilts slightly, and he almost falls to the floor. He wants to get out of here, but he knows that he's had too much to drink. Why not enjoy sitting in this chair a while longer?

He sits back down, thinking that he'll get up and leave in an hour. The time passes slowly, and the booze warmth is gone. A chill in the air eases up his sleeves and pants-legs, so he wraps himself in the sheet that had covered the chair. His eyes droop, and he thinks he should be good to go soon.

He doesn't even realize it when sleep drops over his head like a mask.

CHAPTER NINETEEN

Birds chirp, and Mickey opens his eyes to a room filled with radiant, bright sunshine. The walls are white, and open windows blaze with what could be the dawn of a new day. He blinks several times, and he sees there isn't a ceiling. The walls soar up into the sky, disappearing in the clouds. Something big is flying up there. He squints and thinks it might be a full sized man with wings. An angel?

The light fades, and the walls sink back down. Everything takes the shape they're supposed to have. He's home, and the past is gone. This place is covered with cobwebs and rat shit.

Mickey pushes the cover off of him and nearly jumps when his pint bottle falls out of his lap and thumps on the floor. It doesn't shatter, but his first impulse is to clean it up.

But what's the point? This house is empty and would probably remain so until the foundation rots. Until the wind blows the roof to pieces. Until the walls crumble to dust. Or maybe just whenever some land baron bought the place and razed it for condos.

He picks up the bottle anyway and places it on the mantel over the fireplace where he used to keep a photo of himself and Melissa, smiling and holding hands on the day of their wedding.

He covers the chair again, and he can't help but think that Melissa is gone for good. He's at a dead end. Maybe he should just accept his fate. Hell, is Lucifer Robinson such a bad boss? He's had worse in his life.

It's only a matter of time until Lucifer asks him to kill someone. Is that so bad? Mickey thinks about Sgt. Parker. He remembers Mrs. Parker at the trial and the sick feeling in his guts when the judge declared him not guilty of that particular charge. She cried, and Karnaki put his arm around her shoulders. The look on the federal agent's face was one of pure hatred.

Mickey shakes his head, banishing the memory. It's time to leave.

His stride is slow as he takes one last look around the place. For a moment he thinks he sees himself sitting in his old chair, watching the roiling chaos of flames in the fireplace. The flickering child is back. Boy, girl. Boy, girl. Boy, girl. And there's Melissa coming out of the kitchen. She sits in his lap and reaches her lips to his.

And then it's gone. Nothing remains.

Will he ever see this house again? No, he doesn't think so. This place has seen prettier days, but now it is the empty husk of all his hopes and dreams.

He stands at the front door. The heat has warped the frame, so even though he'd broken it last night, the wood managed to stay in place after he shut it again. He gives it a sharp tug, and it comes open once more.

He takes one step outside before he finds himself looking down twin metal tunnels, and his first impulse is to go for the gun he'd taken off the junkie. It weighs down one side of his jacket, and it sings to be touched, but there is no way he can draw before whoever is pointing the shotgun in his face fires.

Mickey keeps his hands by his sides.

Over the double-barreled shotgun he sees an elderly face. Not geriatric old, but definitely up there. Is this man in his sixties? Probably. But he's in damned good shape. The old man's forearms are bundled masses of muscle, and his hands are banded like iron around the gun. His shaggy white hair goes down to his shoulders without any trace of scalp shining through, thick as a bear's fur. The handlebar mustache over his mouth droops and bristles as if it has a life of its own. Steel blue eyes lock with his own, and only then does he realize that he knows this man.

"Uncle Jack?"

CHAPTER TWENTY

The old man lowers the gun and narrows his eyes. Crows feet explode out from high on his cheeks and open cracks in his leathery skin. His blue eyes traverse Mickey up and down, and only then does a smile grow under the foliage of his mustache.

"Well fuck my shit. Look who it is." He switches the shotgun to his other hand and holds out his right.

Mickey grabs it and shakes with vigor. The strength in Uncle Jack's hand is nearly overpowering, and he has to struggle not to wince.

"Thought you were in the clink," Uncle Jack says. "What are you doing up here?"

"Long story. I can't believe it. You look just the same as when I was a kid. You look tougher than shit."

BLOOD

"If you're going to be a mechanic, you gotta be tough," Jack says. "Not just because you need your strength, but also because you need to make sure some of the lowlifes pay up."

"True."

Jack looks down at Mickey's scarred, gnarled knuckles. "It looks like you might know a bit about lowlifes."

Mickey shrugs. "Shit happens."

"I smell whiskey on your breath. You got some?"

"Nah. I had a pint last night, but I finished it up."

Jack grunts. "You been here all night?"

Mickey nods.

"What for?"

"Just . . . looking."

Jack leans on the shotgun as if it is a walking stick. "I get you. Thinking about everything you had before you were sent up. I guess I would, too."

He reaches into his back pocket and pulls out a flask. "Let's go inside and sit a spell."

Mickey looks at the silver square of stainless steel and steps aside for his uncle. There are very few things he remembers clearly from his youth, but that flask is one of them. Whenever Uncle Jack came over for a visit, he always had the flask with him. It was always filled with whiskey. Back then the smell had been bitter and unpleasant, and Mickey had tried to stay away from it at all costs.

He never thought he would one day be drinking from it. Jack unscrews the top and hands it to his nephew. Mickey thanks him and takes a slug. It's good. Nothing cheap.

Jack finds the bottle on the mantle. "This yours?"

"Yeah."

"Cheap shit, but it'll do the job." Jack takes his flask and belts one back. He sits on the couch without taking the cover off. Dust billows around him, but he doesn't seem to care.

Mickey brushes the sheet aside from his chair and turns it so he can face his uncle. Then he eases back into comfort.

Jack stares at him for a moment, but there's nothing on his face to betray his thoughts. After a moment he chuckles. "Shit. You look almost exactly like Max when he was your age. It's like I'm going back in time. Some of the scars, like the ones on your hands, are even the same."

Mickey has noticed his resemblance to his father several times in the bathroom mirror, usually when shaving on the day after a rough bender. There are few differences. His lips are thinner than Maxwell's, and his ears are far smaller compared to his father's elephant flaps, but the eyes are the same. So is the nose. The hairline is the same, and even the birthmark on his cheek is the same. He wears sideburns to cover it up, but it's there.

Still, it's unsetting for someone else to make note of it.

"Sorry," Jack says. "Didn't mean to get under your skin with that one. It's just that it's disorienting. I have this urge to look in a mirror to make sure I'm still an old man."

Mickey forces himself not to squirm a little. He feels a grimace creep up on his face, but he tries to turn it into a smile. "I haven't seen you in decades. Not since my dad was still alive. Where have you been?"

"That's a hell of a long story," Jack says, "and I don't think I have enough whiskey for it. I've been around, though. Working here, working there, making license plates up at state every once in a while. The usual."

"You did time?"

"Coming from our part of the world, it's hard to go through your entire life without wearing convict orange at some point, right?"

"I guess."

"That's where I was when your ma died. I was doing a stretch for working in a chop shop."

Mickey blinks. "Really?"

"Don't you remember?"

Mickey casts his mind back to his childhood and tries to remember anything about Uncle Jack doing time. Nothing comes up. His mother never discussed it, and by then his father was in the ground.

"You don't remember."

Mickey shakes his head.

"I figured they'd tell you, but I guess I was wrong. In case you don't remember this, either, I was also your godfather. If anything were to happen to your ma, I'd have taken you into my house. Except back then my house was the joint. Hence the orphanage."

The orphanage. Mickey hasn't thought about those days in a long, long time. He thinks about all the hard lessons he learned back then, but more importantly he remembers the hard lessons he taught to his peers. He touches his knuckles, transported back in time.

"You don't remember a lot about your childhood, do you?"

Mickey has never considered this before. Life was rough back in those days, but he doesn't think he's repressing anything. Yet the more he thinks back on his youth, the more gaps he realizes are there. Is there something hiding between the memories? Something plucks at the back of his brain. It's something important, but he can't find it.

"Forget the past," Jack says. "It's not worth remembering. Let's talk about what's happening now, and where we're going. What have you been up to since you got out?"

"Working." Mickey's voice sounds distant, even to himself.

"That don't sound like much fun. Sure, work's important, but so's play. You gettin' any?"

"Any?" Mickey snaps back to attention, but he feels like he's dozed off during a movie, and here he is at the end, confronted with characters he doesn't know and a situation he doesn't understand.

"Pussy," Jack says. "Guy like you, you gotta be lousy with pussy. I know whenever I got out of storage I started hunting for something to stick my dick in."

Mickey clears his throat. "No, actually. I, uh, well . . ."

"Too busy working, you can't find time for pussy? That sucks, kid."

"No, it's not that. It's just . . . have you see Melissa since . . . ?"

Jack takes a healthy slug off the flask and sighs. "I get it now. Sure, I seen her."

Mickey's guts freeze, and his heart hammers against the frost, trying to break through the tundra his body has become. "Do you . . . do you know where she is?"

Jack nods. "I do."

Mickey's hair is suddenly wet, and he runs his finger along the back of his neck. It comes back shining with sweat. "Where is she?"

Jack's hand touches the stock of the shotgun, but he doesn't pick it up. It's a casual motion, not meant to be threatening, just safe. "I don't know if I can tell you that, Mickey. I'm sorry about that, but it's just better that way."

Mickey bares his teeth. They grind together. It makes the inside of his head sound like the belly of a grain mill. "Why is everyone trying to hide her from me? Why is it so important to keep us apart?"

"I don't know what you're talking about. No one's hiding her."

"Bullshit. I hired a private investigator to find her, and he got killed for his trouble. She has no online presence. There are no legal traces of her anywhere. Someone is fucking hiding her from me."

The old man has his hand around the shotgun's stock, and the barrel inches over slightly. It's still far from being aimed at Mickey, but any sudden movement would remedy that. "As far as I know, she's not hiding from anyone, and I hate to say it, kid, but you're starting to rave like a loony. Like maybe you don't know what you're saying."

"I know exactly what I'm saying." Mickey speaks through aching teeth. "You don't know some of the shit I've gone through to find her, and none of it is working out. I used to be a cop, and nothing I can think of is working."

"Then maybe you should tell me how you've been trying to find her," Jack says.

Mickey can feel the wiry hairs on his arms grow. Fangs prickle up out of his gums. He hunches as his clothes strain with building muscle mass. A fuse burns through his guts, waiting to detonate, yet his uncle's tone calms him a bit. Mickey closes his eyes and forces the beast down.

When his heart slows and he's able to unclench his teeth, he tells the whole story from the day the warden let him out to last night. When he's done, he gestures for the flask, and his uncle hands it over. It has been passed back and forth several times during the story, so there is very little left. Mickey drains the last of it off and hands it back.

"Well?"

Jack screws the top back on and slides the flask into his back pocket. "It's one of the stranger tales I've ever heard. And I don't doubt your word, kid, but a guy named Lucifer Robinson? Sounds made up to me, to say nothing of that Lotho guy. I don't care where you come from, you get shot in the head and your ticket's punched."

Mickey shrugs. "I didn't make this up. I mean, I've sometimes thought that this is a weird escape fantasy, and I'm really back in prison. Or maybe I was killed, and this is some kind of horrible afterlife. After all the horrible things I've done, I wouldn't be surprised to find that in my Hell, I've got to go around all the time, taking pay offs and cracking skulls. Forever. Hell, maybe I really did shoot myself all those years ago. Or maybe Karnaki did. I don't know."

"Fuck that shit," Jack says. "I'm alive. Somebody's doing this to you. Who hates you so much that they'd fuck with you like this? Who's got the money for it?"

"A lot of people hate my guts," Mickey says. "Not one of them has the resources for something like this. It's unreasonable."

But something tickles his mind. A thought begging to be born? *Déjà vu.*

"Too bad your brother's dead," Jack says. "He's the only rich guy we know, but there's not much you can do from beyond the grave."

Mickey's breath catches in his throat like a chicken bone. He hasn't thought about Rex in many years, not since after Mickey left the orphanage. He never looked back. He never even cared who might have adopted his brother.

"He was rich?"

Jack's eyebrows shoot up. "You didn't know?"

"I haven't thought about him since . . ." They didn't stick together at the orphanage like regular brothers would have. Mickey had always hated his brother's prissy ways. Rex had a habit of talking too much, and he was really good at finding someone's buttons. Not so good at defending himself, though.

Mickey explains all of this to Jack, who sits back, slightly stunned. "I know you didn't like Rex all that much, but I thought you knew."

"Knew what?"

"Kid, your brother was Rex Paolo, and if the Paolo name ain't rich, I don't know what is."

Rex Paolo? Yes. Mickey has heard the name thousands of times while working the streets. He'd busted Paolo's thugs many times and had stolen drugs from the mobster's dealers only to sell it to other scumbags. He remembered seeing pictures of Paolo, but he'd never recognized him. Could he really be Rex Scarlet?

"How?" Mickey asks. "And why the name change? My brother's as far from a fuckin' Italian as you can get."

"Jesus, kid. Okay, I'm about to say a few things, and I want to apologize ahead of time for it. I know none of this is your fault. It's my asshole brother who did this to you, but I just wanted to say sorry, okay?"

Mickey waits.

"You got a lot of Max in you. More than I'm comfortable with. Believe me, I know how easy it is for a father to beat a beast into a kid, especially the oldest. I'm younger than Max, so he got the brunt of what our own father did to *us*. Goddam, you wouldn't believe the times I've had to tend to my older brother's wounds when we were kids. The old man was a fucking terror."

He pauses. "I know you killed that cop. Vance Parker, I think his name was. Don't worry, I don't have any physical evidence. I guess you could call it spiritual evidence."

Mickey's hands creak, and he forces his fingernails out of his palms. He wants to deny it, but he knows it will do no good.

"I promised I'd never tell anyone, but Max is beyond the law now. One day, when he was old enough to fight back, Max killed our father. Snuck into the bedroom and sawed into his throat with a butcher knife like he was cutting a loaf of bread. Since the old man was a cop—and I doubt that's a coincidence, kid—the authorities figured it was a revenge killing, and Max and I went to the orphanage. Starting to see a pattern?"

Mickey is surprised to find that his hands have balled up again. When did they do that?

"You've got a lot of that animal in you," Jack continues. "I remember what your father was like when the beast—that's what he called it—took over. It really was like watching a man turn into a werewolf, and I'm not ashamed to say it scared the shit out of me. Max never tried anything on me, but maybe that was because I knew well enough to stay out of his way.

"I heard stories about you chopping down trees and shit. I remember that's how Max found a way to channel the beast. He hated it. He wanted to exorcise it. Boxing's how he did it at first, but he hurt too many people doing that. I don't know when he started chopping down trees, but that seemed to do what he wanted. He must have passed that down to you."

Mickey nods.

"I heard about your rep in the orphanage, that you had a habit of kicking the shit out of people. It's a skill I'm sure that came in handy when you were a cop on the streets, putting an extra crack in people's asses. But it was one of the things that kept you in the orphanage until you were eighteen, when they had to let you go. Of course it don't help that you look like an ugly Neanderthal. No offense."

Mickey took none.

"Your brother was a pretty boy, if you recall. And he behaved a lot more than you did. Sure, he had a mouth on him, and he knew how to push everyone's buttons, but he also knew when it was smart to be on his best *et cetera*."

Mickey grunts. "I remember."

"Well, maybe you remember Wallace Paolo. Do you?"

Mickey swayed his flat hand back and forth. "Vaguely."

"Paolo's wife couldn't have kids, and you know how the Eye-talians are about having kids. If you're married and you got none, then it says something about how you ain't a real man. Might even suggest you're a fag, right?"

Mickey nods.

"He needed someone to take over for him someday, so he started shopping around for kids at orphanages. When he found Rex, he knew it had to be him. He was a good kid, good looking, but more importantly he sensed there was something slippery about him, which made him the perfect heir. He took Rex home and gave him a new last name. The rest is history."

"Sounds like he'd have a problem with me," Mickey says. "But you say he's dead."

"That's right. He pissed off the wrong guy and wound up with a Columbian necktie."

"For sure? He's really dead?"

"As dead as they come," Jack says. "Happened when you were inside. It was a big news story for a while."

"He wouldn't fake his own death?"

"He had the money for it, yeah. But a news guy got a hold of some crime scene photos. They blocked out some of the stuff, but it was definitely Rex's body."

"Shit," Mickey says. "I mean, I don't think the things I did to him were bad enough to have him plan out this ridiculously elaborate scheme on me, but still. It would be nice to have something to investigate."

"Well, you tried to kill him on that Thanksgiving. That's cause enough to get revenge."

True. "I haven't really thought about him all that much since that day. I remember once wishing I'd succeeded at killing him. He was a disrespectful, loud-mouthed cocksucker."

Jack stands, leaning on his shotgun. "I guess you can see why I'd be reluctant to tell you where Melissa is. She's got a good life, you know, and I'm pretty sure you'd fuck it up."

The primitive side of Mickey wants to retort, to push the old man back down to the couch, shotgun or not, and to let him know a thing or two.

But Uncle Jack is right. Mickey has an aura of violence around him, and anyone who gets too close is sucked into it to be beaten within an inch of their lives or worse by a force they can't recognize and can never understand.

"I gotta get going, Mickey. A whole day's worth of work is waiting for me back home. I'll give you my number. You ever need anything, you give me a call, all right?"

Jack reaches into his pocket and pulls out a notebook and a pen. He scribbles his number down on a piece of paper.

"My kid," Mickey says. "Is it a boy or a girl?"

Jack pauses and turns his head to look at his nephew. "Shit, you don't know? She never told you?"

"The last time I saw her was at the settlement in

court," Mickey says. "She never even wrote a letter to me."

Jack nods. "It's a girl. Name's Raquel. She's a good kid. Way smarter than we'll ever be."

Mickey's eyes burn, but he knows there will be no waterworks. It feels like the world has beaten all the tears out of him.

Jack hands him the paper. "Give me a call anytime. I'm an old man, and I don't sleep much. My address is on there, too."

Mickey pockets the paper. "Could you at least ask her? Ask her if it's okay for me to see her? It's important."

Jack's face turns to stone. Muscles bulge at both sides of his jaw. "I'll ask. That's all I can promise. Give me your number." He poises his pen to write, and Mickey tells him. "Okay, I'll talk to her, and I'll let you know."

"I just want to see my kid. My *daughter*. I think it's unfair that I don't ever get to meet Raquel."

Jack draws his breath as if he's about to say something, but he pauses.

"What?" Mickey asks.

"Just so you know, Raquel's last name ain't Scarlet. It's Wyrick."

"Wyrick? Why that?"

Jack waits. He doesn't have to say anything. It dawns across Mickey's face, more surprise than anger. He stares off to the fireplace, trying to work his way through it.

"Take care, kid."

Jack walks toward the door, but before he reaches it, he turns. "There's one more thing I wanted you to know. I'm sure it won't ease your mind or anything like that, but I think it's important enough to risk going to jail for."

Mickey continues to stare off into emptiness, but he's still quick to respond. "I'm not a cop anymore. You could tell me anything, and I probably won't care."

"Your old man. My brother. They never solved his murder. That's because I was pretty careful. I thought I could save you and your brother, but I was too late."

Mickey is only mildly surprised. He thinks he should be more shocked by this confession, but there's something about it that makes sense. "Why tell me this?"

"Because the beast lives in me, too. It's just that I learned how to control it better. We're a fucked up family, kid."

CHAPTER TWENTY-ONE

Mickey has a lot to think about on the way home, but he doesn't reach any conclusions by the time he parks the car in front of his apartment. He checks his mailbox on the way in and finds nothing of note.

On his way up the stairs he sees that someone is standing in front of the Jakowskis' door. When he gets closer he recognizes the bald spot at the top of the rotund grizzled man: Arvin Jakowski. At first it looks like he's talking with Melody, who is dressed in a nightgown.

No. They're actually kissing. Arvin rubs his lips all over Melody's face, and she returns the favor. Their tongues wrestle against each other so hard that they coil around one another like twin snakes. The tips wriggle. Both of them stare into Mickey's eyes as he walks by.

He shakes his head. Fucking figures.

He tries to ignore them as he unlocks his door

and heads into the apartment.

*

The next day Mickey looks around online for information about Rex Paolo, just for the hell of it. There are a bunch of news stories, but nothing substantial. He fishes around for Montenegro, too, and finds very little. There are a few archives that have some promising headlines, but they want to charge him for access. He doesn't have a credit card, and he doesn't think it's worth sending away for one.

Besides, libraries are for free. He starts putting on his shoes, but the doorbell buzzes.

Lucifer Robinson. As if it would be anyone else. He playfully jaunts up the stairs with Lotho following him, steady as a rock.

"Good morning, Mr. Scarlet. Fancy meeting you here."

"Lucifer," Mickey says. "Come on in." He steps aside, and Lucifer all but dances across the threshold.

"It's a beautiful day, isn't it?"

Mickey is almost amused enough to smile. "You seem cheerful. Get laid last night?"

"I *did*, as a matter of fact, but that's not why I'm so happy. A number of events have come together in such a way as to illuminate my near future."

"Pussy and money. You must have had quite the night."

"Ah! Money. Yes, cash has a great deal to do with my mood today, but never mind that. The powers that be have decided that you have earned a special place in our hierarchy. Of course, it will include more duties, but we feel certain that you'll be up to it."

Mickey can see that Lucifer is lost in whatever pleasure he gets out of this kind of thing. Time to hit him hard. Mickey smiles wide enough to show off his wisdom teeth. "That's great, buddy. Have you found Melissa Wyrick yet?"

"So sorry, Mr. Scarlet. The task is a bit harder than we'd initially thought. Your ex-wife's current location is still evasive, but we're working on it."

Interesting. It zipped right past Lucifer. Good.

"Just thought I'd ask," Mickey says. "I take it you have a job for me, then?"

"Absolutely. Lotho, give him the file."

The person in the folder this time is no mere junkie or gambler. This is a police officer, some kid by the name of Sawyer Fenton. From what Mickey can tell, this officer is a crusader on the very first rung of what looks to be a long ladder. The arrests this kid has to his name reads like a who's-who of the underworld, and it looks like a lot of it is going to stick.

Many of the people he's putting in prison used to work for Rex Paolo.

"You want me to put the frighteners into this guy?" Mickey asks. But he knows the answer already.

"No, Mr. Scarlet. We expect you to kill Officer Fenton."

Show time. Mickey slaps the folder against Lucifer's skinny chest and holds it in place with the tips of his fingers. "What did I tell you before? I don't kill anyone."

Lotho steps forward, but Lucifer waves him

off. "I recall exactly what you said. I'd like to call your attention to Sgt. Parker, though."

Mickey snarls. "You think you understand me? I ought to fucking twist your pretty little head off and stick it in your dickhole."

A shadow falls across the both of them. Mickey sees from the corner of his eye that it's Lotho. He's taller than ever before, and he blocks out the sunlight from the windows. His fists are bigger than Mickey's head, and his mouth is a jagged buzzsaw of piranha teeth. He cracks his massive knuckles, and it sounds like tree limbs breaking in a tornado.

"Mr. Robinson?" he asks. His voice is a guttural lion purr.

"You're making Lotho nervous, Mr. Scarlet." The ever present grin floats on Lucifer's face almost with a life of its own.

Mickey releases the folder, and the whole thing falls to the floor. Papers spread out all over Lucifer's feet. "I'm out."

Lucifer glances at the puddle of papers around his shoes, and he steps back, letting them slump down into a pile. "Are you sure you're willing to give up everything you've worked for? Just to avoid doing something you've done at least once?"

"You don't know that I killed Parker," Mickey says. "Only I do."

"You killed him, all right. Have you forgotten who we are?"

Mickey turns away, grabbing his face, hoping that Lucifer thinks he's trying to hide tears.

"Killing is always hardest the first time," Lucifer continues. "I cannot count the number of people I've sent to their graves, shallow or otherwise. The first time tore me apart, but the second time was just as easy as swatting a fly."

There's something odd in his voice, and Mickey suspects he's lying. Lucifer *loves* murder, and he always has.

"Why not just try it?" Lucifer asks.

Mickey swallows and hopes enough phlegm gets into this one. "Because my soul is black enough."

"Face it, Mr. Scarlet. You're already going to Hell. What's one more sin?"

Mickey rubs his eyes until they burn. They feel red enough. He turns back to face Lucifer. "Your mother named you very well. But there's some people who can't be tempted." He reaches into his pocket and throws his keys down at Lucifer's feet, where they bounce into a nest of papers.

Lucifer blinks. "Ten thousand dollars. That's the money my boss told me I could use to help convince you."

"Not good enough. I'll be out of here by dawn tomorrow." He starts to walk toward the kitchen.

Lucifer sighs. "Fine. Walk out on us. Throw it all away. But if you give up now, you'll never see your wife and child again."

Mickey whirls on Lucifer and grabs him by his white lapels. He thrusts the pallid man against the wall and snarls in his face. For a moment Mickey thinks he might not be acting anymore. It feels too real. It feels like the beast.

Too late to back down now.

"You motherfucker. You knew where she was all this time, and you pretended you didn't know shit."

Lucifer gags, but he is prevented from speaking by Mickey's thick knuckles digging heavily against his Adam's apple.

Lotho slips a hand under Mickey's armpit and presses two fingers against a nerve. Mickey yelps and involuntarily releases Lucifer's jacket. Lotho hurls him backwards, and his head connects with the wall. His vision blurs for a moment, but it isn't the first time he's had his skull cracked. He blinks, shakes his head and the world comes back into focus.

Lucifer leans against the wall, rubbing his throat. Loose strands of his hair hang in his face. "You're right. I know exactly where she is. And if you don't get your ass in line, you're never going to find her."

Time to let the act drop. Mickey rubs the back of his head. "Sure. I'll do it. But if I don't get any information out of you when I'm finished, I'm going to kill you. And there's nothing Lotho can do to save you."

Lucifer straightens his tie and tries to slap the wrinkles out of his jacket. It doesn't work. "I'll check on you tomorrow evening. Officer Fenton had better be dead by then."

Mickey watches from the floor as Lucifer and Lotho head for the door. As soon as they're gone he stands and gets a bottle from the kitchen. He takes a drink to help ease the throb in his head but only one. After that he puts his shoes and jacket on and heads for the library.

*

Mickey tries to remember the last time he set

187

foot in a public library, and he can't. It had to be when he was a kid for some school project or other. He isn't prepared for the changes. They no longer have card catalogues since all that information is now on computers. Oddly, they're still called card catalogues.

A lot more is permissible in the library, too. There is no longer a need for absolute silence as the clacking of keyboards fill the air and a background of low conversation from students in study groups buzzes.

Mickey doesn't know if these things are good, and he catches himself. He doesn't want to sound too much like Willie Salas.

At least this place doesn't have all the dust that the prison library had. While it had been a pretty quiet location filled with cons reading law books and trying to figure out how to appeal their cases, the dust caused a constant chatter of sneezes, and nobody cared enough to grab a duster and get to work.

Mickey has a bit of trouble locating the periodicals section, but when he does the clerk is able to help him navigate the catalogue for the articles he needs.

He's not surprised when Lucifer Robinson's name doesn't come up, but he's grateful when he finds what he needs about Anthony Montenegro and Rex Paolo. He goes back a little further to see if the elder Paolo is mentioned in the press, but he finds little he doesn't already know.

The catalogue gives him reference numbers for the rolls of microfilm he needs, so he writes them down and takes them to the clerk.

"Sit here, sir." The clerk points to a vacant

microfilm reader. One of two, both unused. "I'll be right back."

"Sure."

This is the only piece of equipment that has dust on it. It's a thin layer, but it's still there. Perhaps he's the first person in a year to whip through the past on this war-beaten steed.

The clerk returns with several boxes of microfilm, which he places on the table next to the machine. "Do you know how to use one of those?" he asks.

Mickey nods. "It's been a while, but I'm familiar."

"Good. When you're done, just put them back in the boxes and leave them in the basket on my desk, okay?"

"Sure."

There isn't much to say about Wallace Paolo. It's clear that there were a lot of suspicions floating around the guy, but no one ever had enough evidence to arrest him. The feds even took a shot at him by using the old Capone gambit: they went over his taxes with a fine-tooth comb, and everything appeared to be legit. It seemed that Paolo was invincible.

Until lung cancer took him out fifteen years ago. The obituary mentions Rex, but there is no mention of him being adopted. It's never brought up in any of these articles.

Mickey comes upon a picture of a restaurant opening on the west side. There's Rex Paolo. He grew up to be a very handsome man. Or maybe a pretty boy. He looks soft and delicate as ever. Hollywood looks. There is a lot of their mother in that face. A lot of quiet beauty. None of the hard, gnarled features of Maxwell Scarlet are present on his face, but he does have incredibly large hands. They're straightening his tie as he laughs with some pretty young thing. She looks like she's barely out of high school.

The suit looks nice. So does the pinkie ring and the cuff links. Rex was very well taken care of in life.

Mickey tries to envision his hands around Rex's throat again. It's too easy.

After reading more he discovers that Rex had inherited millions of dollars on paper. Who knows how much he actually had? He also had the luck of his adoptive father. Lots of accusations, no arrests.

It turns out that Montenegro was his uncle. He helped Rex take his $789 million dollar inheritance and invest it very shrewdly. Mickey can't believe the number he's looking at. Could Rex have really been worth $56 billion?

Again, Mickey thinks of the cash that probably went unreported. He can't believe such a wealthy man existed, much less that he was Mickey's brother. Anyone with that amount of money can do whatever they want. They can bribe every cop in the country for that. Hm. They can also bribe a prison warden. And Karnaki. And God knows who else.

Is it possible . . . ? No. Mickey can't bring himself to think Rex wanted revenge against him for such a petty thing. But if he did, is it not reasonable that Uncle Montenegro would be willing to carry out such a plan after Rex's death?

$56 billion. Jack said that he'd seen photos of Rex's dead body. Mickey can't shake the feeling that someone with that much money can easily fake his own death.

Mickey looks back at the restaurant picture. The image of Rex seems otherworldly compared to his surroundings, like a ghost among the living. It winks at him.

He reads more. So much more that the words start to blur in front of him. They slowly melt into a face yawning in horror. Or maybe hunger. It presses out of the screen, but he barely registers it. He's lost in his research. Sometimes he has to remind his lungs to breathe.

He finds a picture of Rex's mansion on the north side. It's massive. A palace. In life Rex was single, and according to gossip columns he fucked everything with a pussy. Yet he clearly had no intention of starting a family. Rex lived alone in that gargantuan castle. He had servants, but only one butler and one assistant was on duty at all times.

At first Mickey thinks this is wasteful, but when he really thinks about it, what can a man with so much money do with his riches? There are only so many charities one can contribute to before realizing there is still so much money one can spend. Why not buy an absurdly large mansion?

And Rex did contribute to charities. He had a fundraiser at least every weekend, and he always made a show of his donations. There was even a foundation named after him. He was a politically interested individual and helped out candidates whenever he could. Mickey wonders what he got in return.

Here's a picture of Rex shaking hands with the

previous president of the United States. Both have giant grins on their faces. Masks of jollity. Rex clasps the president's hand in both of his as if to say, "I own you, motherfucker." There are seas of balloons and waves of confetti around them. Mickey hears the faint music of the band. It's "Hail to the Chief." He touches the screen, and his hand comes away with shreds of confetti. He brushes them off and watches as Rex winks yet again. The handshake moves up and down like three seconds of time caught in a loop.

Enough. He leans back in his chair and rubs his eyes. When he looks again, the picture is static.

Time to move on to the Montenegro stuff. Before he can, his cell phone rings. An old lady going through a red-bindered issue of *House and Garden* looks at him over her reading glasses. She makes a clucking sound in her throat and shakes her head.

"Sorry," he says. *Guess some things about libraries are the same.* He answers the phone, shuffling away from the microfilm reader. "This is Mickey."

"It's Uncle Jack. How are you?"

Mickey finds a niche between the newspaper racks. No one loiters around him. "I'm fine. Do you have news for me?"

"I talked with Melissa and stated your case. It wasn't an easy thing to do, you know."

"I do, and I appreciate it." Mickey's heart rate shoots up so quickly he can feel it throb through every inch of his body. A thought loop passes through his brain, and it says "please" over and over again.

"I finally convinced her to meet with you. She

wants to see you at your old place tonight. Seven. Okay?"

Mickey can't find his voice, and he can only hear the thunder of his own pulse in his head. A hot flash blazes across his skin, and he feels a cold trickle of sweat drip down his spine.

"Mickey? You there?"

He croaks, then clears his throat. "Yeah, I'm here. My daughter will be there, too, right?"

"Yep. I should give you a fair warning, though. Melissa's man is going to be there, too. She says for protection, although I'm pretty sure you can take him if it comes to that."

Mickey thinks he should be upset by this last part, but he isn't. He's just glad he can finally meet his daughter. *His daughter!*

"Thank you very much, Uncle Jack. I can't tell you how much I'm grateful."

"Don't be grateful. Just don't fuck it up, okay? Don't come dragging her and her family into your world. Understand?"

"I'd never do that."

"Okay. I'll tell her you'll be there. So long, kid."

Mickey hangs up and holds the phone in a tremulous hand, staring at the blank screen. Can this be real? Is he finally going to see Melissa and his daughter tonight?

He looks at the clock. It's nearly four-thirty, so he has plenty of time to get Raquel a present. What should he get her, though? What kind of person is she? Is she too old for dolls? Too young for books? Is she a princess or a tom boy?

First things first. He's got to put the microfilm back and give Lucifer a call. The mystery no longer matters to him. It's time to quit for real. Lucky for Sawyer Fenton.

He goes back to the microfilm reader and puts everything back in their respective boxes. He stops by the clerk's desk to drop them off and say thanks.

The clerk doesn't look up for a moment. When he does, he seems timid. His posture is too stiff. His nose has shrunk and is mousy. Blackness fills his eyes. Long whiskers on his cheeks twitch. "You're welcome." Even his voice is squeaky.

An alarm goes off in Mickey's brain and flows through his body, causing his skin to tingle and the hair at the back of his neck to stand up. Adrenaline surges. His street sense kicks in, and he looks up into the curved mirror behind the clerk's desk.

No one is behind him.

Paranoia? Instinct?

Maybe. But his street sense has never let him down before.

He takes his notebook and heads down the stairs to the ground floor. As he makes his way to the doors, the feeling intensifies. His body becomes a radar beacon, sending out waves as feelers. They hit several people and send back their echoes. None of them look suspicious. Just patrons.

Before he steps outside he sees from the corner of his eye a Raggedy Ann doll. It sits on the checkout counter, not a Raggedy Andy in sight. A small price tag sticks out from her leg. Ten bucks.

What girl doesn't like Raggedy Ann?

He makes a detour and picks up the doll. The desk clerk, a young girl about twenty years of age, smiles. "It's a classic. Everyone loves the classics."

"Ain't that the truth," Mickey says. "I'll take her."

The clerk scans the barcode. "Daughter?"

"Yeah."

"How old is she?"

"Seven." *I think.* Maybe she's eight. Math was never his strong suit. Hell with it. Short answers are always the best answers.

"I have a niece that age," the clerk says. "It's such an adorable age, you know?"

"Sure."

"Sometimes I wish I could have been seven forever. The world seemed so much simpler back then."

Mickey thinks about when he'd been seven. He tries not to shake his head.

"That'll be ten dollars."

Mickey's eyebrows slip up his forehead. "No tax?"

"Libraries don't charge tax."

He hands over the cash and thanks her. Doll in hand, he heads for the doors.

Outside he feels safe enough to turn off his inner detector. He remains wary, but if someone is going to do something, they probably would have done it already. Maybe his imagination just got carried away with itself.

When he's fifteen feet away from his car, pulling the key ring out of his pocket, someone calls out:

"Mickey Scarlet!"

The voice has a great deal of authority in it, and Mickey drops his notebook, shifting Raggedy Ann to his left hand so he can reach into his right pocket for the junkie's gun.

He turns toward the person, and his guts chill over. It isn't some mob leg-breaker or anything like that; it's a pair of cops, both with their hands on their guns. Not drawn, but they're a pussy hair away from turning the library parking lot into the OK Corral.

There's no way he can clear his pocket in time.

Mickey relaxes, letting both hands fall into view. Raggedy Ann dangles by his side. "Can I help you?"

"You're going to have to come with us," one of them says. His skin is bright pink, and he's very tall. His nose is squat, a pig's nose. It's hard to see his eyes through the mirrored sunglasses he wears, but the ghost of them looks beady.

It takes Mickey a moment to realize that the other one is identical to the first. They're twins.

"If you know my name, then you know Lucifer Robinson's name."

"Oh, we know him, all right," the other says. "Come with us."

So the gloves are off. Does Lucifer really have spies everywhere? The clerk didn't look like much, but Mickey's guts tell him that the mousy bastard had ratted him out. At least there's one thing going in Mickey's favor: he's finally going to get some answers.

He stoops down for his notebook.

"Leave it. Just come with us."

Mickey shrugs. He doesn't need it anymore. "Fine. Where are we going?"

"You'll find out."

Mickey follows them.

INTERLUDE

For the past two years, Ralph Karnaki got to ride a desk instead of being out in the field. This made him gain weight, and it reduced the chances of him getting shot, but more importantly he got his own private office. He sits there now, sweating with only the desk light on. The rest of the room is concealed in shadows.

He likes his office because he can hide a bottle of whiskey in here, far away from prying eyes. He doesn't keep it in his drawer—rookie move—but he never has to go too far. All he has to do is roll his chair over to the bookcase, slip a few law books aside and pull out a fifth of booze, usually bourbon.

He takes a pull off the bottle, then another, and puts it back. He's been doing this a lot more since his visit from Lucifer Robinson. He knows someone will eventually catch him, and he wants to stop doing it, but he can't stop thinking about

Mickey Scarlet living free. All Karnaki has to do is blow the whistle, but he can't bring himself to do it. He tries to think that the money will make everything fine, but it doesn't. It won't make the painful twinge in his guts go away.

He scoops some peanut butter into his mouth. It's a trick he learned from an alcoholic. Mints don't hide the stink of whiskey. The only thing that can fool even an AA group is peanut butter.

Karnaki is about to dive into an underling's report when his cell phone goes off in his pocket. It's against regulation to have anything other than a standard ring tone, but there is one kind of call he always wants to be aware of: a Mickey Scarlet call. This is what he hears now.

He pushes a button and presses the phone to his ear close enough to feel the sweat around his temple squish against it. "Hello?"

"This is Decker. Remember how you wanted to know if the cops ever made a move against Mickey Scarlet?"

"Yes."

"And it's worth a couple of hundred?"

"The check's as good as in the mail, just as long as the info's good. What do you have?"

There is a pause. "Okay, they put an APB out for him earlier today. The cops got a tip from a library clerk that Scarlet was going through a bunch of old microfilm, and that he was looking at them right now."

Another pause. "Go head," Karnaki says.

"The cops picked him up there."

"Which officers?"

"A guy named Collins, and the other guy is Breuer, I think. They got Scarlet in the back of their cruiser right now." And then he tells Karnaki where they're going.

A chill runs through Karnaki's body. Yes. This is what he's been waiting for ever since he visited Mickey's apartment. His body tingles with anticipation. He's worried he might drop the phone.

"Thank you. I'll make sure you get paid."

"You got my name, right?"

"Yes, yes. Decker." He hangs up the phone and looks up Collins and Breuer in the FBI system. A quick read reveals two shady cops. No evidence, but a lot of coincidences. He is sure they're working for Lucifer Robinson.

He needs another drink. Brushing the books aside, he yanks the bottle out of its hidey-hole and slugs down three shots of whiskey. This is for real. It's finally time.

He opens another law book. This one is hollowed out in the middle, and there rests his old throw-down piece and six bullets. The office job negates his need for it, but he never got rid of it. Who knows when someone would need an unregistered firearm?

His fingers shake as he loads the gun and puts it in his coat pocket. He then picks up his phone and looks through his contacts until he finds her name. He hits dial and waits to hear her voice.

It only takes one ring. "Ralph. Is it time?"

"Yes."

"Finally."

He gives her the details, and she listens. After, he tells her where to meet him, and they both hang up.

Karnaki turns off the desk lamp, and the entire

office goes dark. He sits there for a moment in the silence, and he can't help but smile. He always knew redemption would feel wonderful, but he didn't understand just how transformative it really is.

He gets up and leaves. He tells no one where he's going.

CHAPTER TWENTY-TWO

Neither cop searches Mickey, and they make no move to handcuff him. Instead they open the back of their cruiser and gesture to him. This breach of protocol startles him. They obviously know about how dangerous he is. Why would they not fully detain him?

It occurs to him that they might want to hold on to him for a long time. Maybe forever. Which means he's going to miss his date with Melissa tonight.

Something crawls in his guts, and it isn't the beast. This time it's just sickness.

He sits at the edge of the seat so his face is all but pressed against the cage. "Hey, is it okay if we can put this off?"

"Why? Got somewhere else to be?" The cop chuckles.

Mickey almost blushes at the stupidity of the comment, but it's something he had to say. He thinks back to his time as a cop and wonders how many times he'd heard something similar from a criminal. How many times he'd responded the same way. "It's pretty important, actually."

"So is this," the other cop says. His tone is no-nonsense and impatience. "Sit back, sir."

There is nothing else to do or say. Mickey slides further into the Plexiglas seat and waits. The world flows by outside the windows.

"Either of you guys married?" Mickey asks.

"Sure," the driver says. His partner immediately says, "Fuck off."

"Come on, what's the harm?" the driver says. "What else do we have to do?" He turns slightly to glance at Mickey. "Yeah, I'm married."

The other cop remains silent.

"Kids?" Mickey asks.

"Two. Boy and a girl."

"I was married," Mickey says. "When I was in jail my wife divorced me. I have a kid, too, but I've never met her. She's about seven years old, and I only just found out her name. Could you imagine that?"

"Shit no," the driver says. "Sucks, bro."

"We're not dropping you off anywhere," his partner says. "I don't care about your life story. We've been paid in advance, and I'm not going to give that money back because of some sob story."

"Well, yeah," the driver says. "There's no way, but still. That's pretty harsh."

Mickey fingers the outline of the junkie's gun in his jacket pocket, and he wonders what they would do if he drew down on them now. But what good will that do? Even if he shot them both, how the fuck would he get out of the back of the cruiser? They'd crash, and if he tried to shoot out the windows, the bullets would ricochet off them and probably cut him to pieces.

He just has to ride this out. Then, when their guard is down, he can drill them both and take the cruiser out to his old house to meet his daughter.

A small, niggling part at the back of his brain didn't like the idea of shooting cops. He'd never kill them unless he had to, but wounding them would be bad enough. Ah, fuck them. They're between Mickey and his daughter.

Raggedy Ann sits next to him, looking at her hands folded in her lap. She looks like she might want to be with Raggedy Andy rather than here.

The cop riding shotgun turns on the radio and jerks the volume knob up until the sound of some right wing talk show host fills the entire cruiser. He's on a tear about something he had probably supported when the president had been a Republican.

The ride is long, and after a while they leave the city. Not out to the boonies where Mickey's old house is, but into rich territory. They pass monolithic houses, houses so decadent that they should contain entire families and not just one. Houses where the owners probably have not been in every room. Houses that cost more money than the average joe makes in a lifetime.

They take a turn, and the rich neighborhood recedes. There is a lot more space out here where the ultra rich live. Acres of land surround their mansions, most of it shielded by brick walls with barbed wire at the top.

It's suddenly hot in the cruiser, and Mickey unbuttons his shirt slightly so a v of his wiry chest hair pokes out. He has the sensation that they're driving down a hill, but he doesn't see the evidence through the windows. Soon the walls turn redder and redder until they start dancing. They're flames licking at the burgundy sky. Through them he can see that they're no longer passing mansions; they're passing medieval castles.

On the other side of the road he sees what looks like a sea of jerking, sweaty flesh. It's an orgy of people with horns and forked tongues. Their penises are massive, and their vaginas are gaping caves covering their entire bodies. They ululate to the sound of mournful, heavy music like a metal ballad with no words. It's being played by a small band of musicians. One of them plays a violin made from a femur bone and stretched nerves. Another plays a cello made from a human torso. The drums are skulls, and the singer performs like a tenor with three heads. All of their throats are fluted deeply, exposing their insides very clearly. So is the rib cage.

They drive past another property, and a drooling slob with folds of fat that hang down to the ground cracks a whip. About twenty people, all faceless and naked, toil at building his castle, and the slow ones are quickly lashed to the bone.

The road has transformed into row upon row upon row of screaming, writhing bodies. Bones crackle as the tires pass over them. Approaching from the front Mickey sees another fat bastard, this one with the features of a pig, much like the two cops. He is borne on a sedan chair by four of the faceless wretches. There is a headless woman with her breasts bared sitting next to him. He fondles them while she feeds him eyeballs.

"We're almost there," the driver says.

Mickey closes his eyes, banishing these horrible visions. There is nothing to filter out the screams, though. He feels very tired, and he wishes that this was already over. Even if it ends in his death at the hands of whoever pulls Lucifer's strings.

They pull up to a wrought iron gate with giant spikes at the top. All but three of them have screaming people skewered to them through their anuses. Their cries of torment are garbled because of the pointy ends sticking out of their mouths. Shit and blood smear the gate below them.

The driver reaches out the window and presses a button. He speaks for a moment through the intercom, but Mickey can't understand it. It's another language, kind of like German if it sounded even meaner.

The gate creaks open, dragging the victims into a large stone slot, scraping some of their limbs off. They fall wetly to the ground, and the cop drives over them. The cruiser hops a couple of times.

The driveway is long and paved with more unfortunate howling souls. They're surrounded by gentle quiet flames interrupted every once in a while by a statue. It takes Mickey a moment to realize that the statues are actually scenes depicting people being tortured in devices from the middle ages.

There are gnarled stony trees everywhere, and they all have many people hanging from nooses from every branch. They twitch and moan, but most of the strength has gone out of them.

Dark things dart among the flames. They're shadows at first, but finally one of them slows down long enough for Mickey to get a good look at it. He thinks it's a dog at first, but its eyes are glowing red and two thick bull-like horns juts from its massive head. It's about as big as a lion, and its claws would look at home on a gargoyle. It flashes its teeth, and they look like an elephant's tusks.

At the end of the drive is a circle, and in the middle is a fountain of blood. An ancient Greek statue stands in the middle spouting blood from his eyes, mouth, nose and a deep slit in his throat. Something swims in the bowl, but it's too dark to see whatever monstrous thing lived in that kind of environment.

The cop car pulls up to the front door where Lucifer Robinson waits, leaning on his cane. At his side is Lotho, and in the guard's large hands is a knot of leashes. Four hell beasts strain at the end of them, growling at the car.

There's no way Mickey can shoot the cops and get away now. If he made a move, Lotho would unleash those monsters, and then he'd never get to see Melissa and his daughter. He's stuck, and that's that.

Lucifer glides down the steps and throws an envelope through the open passenger side window. "Thank you, Collins. You and your partner are ever-efficient. I hope you enjoy your bonus."

"Pleasure," Collins—the passenger—says. He makes the envelope disappear into his uniform. "He's all yours."

Lucifer opens the door and steps back, bowing

deeply and sweeping his hand out. "Mr. Scarlet."

Mickey gets out and stretches his legs. He reaches back in for Raggedy Ann and stuffs her in his pocket. Finally, he looks around at the screaming, the misery, the fire and torture and turns his gaze back to the pallid gentleman. "*Lucifer.*"

Lucifer chuckles. "I know. I know. It's not what it seems. I assure you that I'm not the devil. Never have been, never will be."

And he seems so sincere.

"What's with the cops?" Mickey asks. "I'm supposed to be busy killing Sawyer Fenton, right?"

"He can wait. Someone wants to see you very badly."

There's no bullshitting him. Mickey had probably never even put one over on him. "What tipped you off?"

"The comment you made in the apartment," Lucifer says. "I wasn't entirely sure, but when you went to the library instead of to Fenton's favorite hangout, I knew you'd figured it out. My master had a much better cat-and-mouse game planned, but he thought that since the surprise was spoiled, it was time for the endgame. Follow me."

So Lucifer doesn't know that Mickey doesn't have all the pieces yet. This is much more aggravating. When Lucifer turns, Mickey ponders the idea of putting a bullet in the back of his head. Lotho would probably unleash the hell beasts, but it might be worth it if only to wipe the omnipresent smirk off Lucifer's cultured face.

"Don't even think about it," Lucifer says.

"What?"

"Ben Fulton's gun. Leave it in your pocket."

Mickey feels a chill settle in. Lucifer is a creepy fucker, but is he capable of mind reading? Or had he watched as Mickey pounded the shit out of that junkie and took his gun? The right side of his jacket hangs a bit low, so it could be a matter of simple deduction.

Lucifer passes the roaring hell dogs without glancing at them. Mickey gives them a wide berth, and when they jump toward him, he involuntarily takes a step back. In the center of the half-ring of beasts Lotho stands motionless. His arms don't strain at the act of holding them at bay. Mickey can see himself reflected in the guard's round sunglasses. The reflection of his head looks larger than anything else as his body trails out behind him, very small. His face is like a balloon held to the ground by the string of his body. He looks fragile, and for all of his toughness he feels it, too.

Mickey enters the house through the large double doors and finds himself in a foyer with what he first takes to be plants that are on fire. Then he realizes they're actually fire, and they move like they're alive. Paintings adorn the wall, each depicting mutilated bodies with their insides spread open almost like autopsy photos. An elaborate chandelier of flames flickers from its hook above.

Lucifer leads him through a series of corridors until they come to the dining room. The table is about the size of an Olympic swimming pool, and it dominates the room. It's made of bones. There is food on every square inch of it, and it's all Thanksgiving themed. A giant turkey sits directly in the middle of the smorgasbord.

There are only two chairs, though, and both have places set for them: one at the head and one at the foot.

A wall slides out of sight, and a platform hovers out. An orchestra of living corpses is on it, and their instruments are all made of body parts, like the band Mickey had seen on the drive here. They break out into a majestic song, something that might be used when you die and meet God. Bass flows through Mickey's chest, and though he feels like he's reached the end of his life, he can't help but be impressed.

A panel opens in the cathedral ceiling, and a plank lowers to the right. A figure stands on it, motionless and staring straight ahead. He has no skin or clothes, but it looks like a bloody tie is hanging from under his throat. A cloak of flames hangs down his back, and a crown of gold and bones rests on top of his head. His eyes glow yellow and seem empty. Sheaves of money rain around him. They squirm as if alive, and when they touch the marble floor, they curl up and turn into cinders.

The plank comes to a rest by the head of the table. The skinless man steps down and turns his attention to Mickey. Up close, Mickey can see a hole in the man's forehead, and blood dribbles from it, forming an upside down V around his nose.

The music stops. The orchestra retreats back into the wall.

The man flashes his shockingly white teeth, and they look like they should be on a piranha. He makes a garbled sound, then shakes his head. He grabs the tie and shoves it into a slit in his throat. He reaches into his mouth to fish it through, and Mickey realizes that it's actually his tongue.

A Columbian necktie.

Oh shit.

"Recognize me?" the skinless man asks.

Mickey doesn't, but he looks at the turkey and has a pretty good idea.

"Allow me to slip into something more comfortable."

He gestures to the money that still floats to the floor. Hundred dollar bills flutter to him and surround him in a flurry. The fire cloak is extinguished with a hiss, and smoke eases up to the ceiling. Through the flurry, Mickey can see a very expensive suit forming. He can see skin bubbling up on the man's hands. When the rest of it clears, the skinless man has a face, too. A very handsome face.

Rex Paolo.

"I'm glad you could come, brother," he says. "Jesus Christ, you look just like Dad. If I didn't know that old bastard was a pile of bones, I'd think you were him."

"I'd say you look like Mom," Mickey says, "but you lost a lot of her. Right now I don't know what you look like."

Rex laughs. It is a cruel, empty sound. "Maybe it's the way I comb my hair."

"You sound nothing like her, though. I think you've been calling me."

"I think I've been, too."

"Can we cut the shit and get to the point? I have something important to do tonight. I know you want some kind of weird revenge thing from me, but I don't understand this game you're playing. Let's just get it out of the way so we never have to see each other again."

Rex's face shifts, and it melts slowly down his skull for a moment. He pushes it back into place with the delicate tips of his fingers. "You have *two* important things to do tonight. But you're thinking about seeing Melissa and Raquel, right?"

Mickey doesn't bother to answer.

"I've gotten to know them a bit," Rex says. He reaches into his pocket and pulls out a gold cigarette case, a twin to the one Lucifer has. "Smoke?"

"No."

Rex lights up, and he takes his time with it. "You really fucked them over, you know? Not as bad as you did me, but still. I don't think you're ever going to be in their good graces, and to be perfectly honest, I don't think you deserve to be."

The beast smiles in Mickey's guts. A drop of sweat runs down the back of his head to his collar. His hands itch, and he wonders what it would be like to chop his brother down like a tree. "Save it. I'm seeing them tonight, and there's nothing you can do to stop me."

"I think it's pretty funny," Rex says. "They loved the hell out of me. Little Raquel loved it when Uncle Rex came by for a visit. But she doesn't think much of you. You're too much like the old man, and it shows. Kids see these things."

Mickey's hands curl up on their own, and he steps forward without thinking about it.

Rex doesn't so much as flinch.

Mickey doesn't get far. Lucifer gently touches his neck with a gold-plated derringer. No words are spoken, but Mickey stops.

"Make no mistake about it, brother," Rex says. "I'm going to kill you tonight. That's the other important thing, the one you didn't think about. You're never going to meet Raquel. Violent fucks like you don't even deserve to have wonderful daughters like her."

Mickey sneers. "So you're a protector, huh? What about all those young women you hooked on smack and then forced into prostitution? Or the guys you ordered to be killed, guys like Sawyer Fenton? Can't hurt the bottom line, can you?"

"Don't get self-righteous. It doesn't suit you. When you were on the police force, you did a lot of the same shit, and if you didn't do it yourself, your actions caused it to happen."

Mickey's teeth rumble against each other, and it sounds like an earthquake in his head. "At least I never killed anyone."

Rex smiles. "That's funny. Maybe we should ask Vance Parker."

Mickey glares at him, but he doesn't say anything.

"Poor Sgt. Parker. His wife still grieves him, and she curses your name every night before she goes to bed. I know because I kept close to her before, well." He draws a finger across his throat. "You know. She thought I was a good guy no matter what the papers said because we went to the same church. She once offered me her life savings, all two thousand of it, to have you killed. Can you believe that?"

"You take it?" Mickey asks. "I figure if you're going to do it, you might as well profit off of it."

"Killing you is its own reward," Rex says. "I

turned her down. I'm the good guy from church, remember?"

Rex turns around and sits at the head of the table. Mickey notices a grandfather clock behind his brother. It's about six. One hour to go. He can still make it, if only he could get the fuck out of here.

Rex sees him looking at the clock. "I moved that back there so you could see it. So you could know that you'd never be able to make it out to Melissa in time. And then, just as the clock strikes seven, I'm going to kill you."

Lucifer presses the gun against Mickey's throat. "I'll take Fulton's gun now."

Mickey inches into his pocket and very slowly draws out the pistol by the butt. Lucifer snaps it up, and the derringer comes away. It's still pointed at Mickey, but it no longer jabs at him.

Rex gestures to the other end of the table. "Have a seat, brother. It's time for your last meal, and I only thought it fitting that it should be Thanksgiving turkey."

Mickey makes his way to his seat like a toy robot, the kind that needs to be wound up. His gait is stiff, and it looks like he could easily fall down. He brushes the ash from the money, which still falls like snowflakes, from the chair and sits down. He sees a bottle of whiskey in front of him and a thick whiskey glass next to it. The seal is unbroken, and the quality is phenomenal. It's the kind of alcohol Mickey used to fantasize about when he was a broke twenty-something.

He places Raggedy Ann next to his plate. It looks like she's an invited guest.

On the other side of the table, Rex reaches into

his suit and pulls out a .45 semi-auto. It's very shiny and very large. Mickey could easily see himself getting shot by this gun. The exit wound would not leave much.

Rex puts the gun next to his plate. "Lucifer? Would you do the honors?"

Lucifer nods, and he puts the derringer in his pocket. Mickey's gun goes on the table next to the turkey, well out of reach.

As Lucifer carves the bird, Rex pours wine into a glass. Mickey breaks the seal on the bottle with a butter knife and pulls the cork. The whiskey splashes into his glass, and he makes sure to pour a very tall drink. If this is indeed going to be his last hour on earth, he wants to at least have a bellyful of good booze.

But he only sips at it. Not enough to equal a half-shot. He wants to still have his senses about him. He figures he'll need them.

As soon as their plates are full, Rex glances up at Lucifer. "You may leave us."

Lucifer cocks a pale eyebrow. "Are you sure?"

"There's nothing my brother can to do harm me. He has no weapons, and if he starts moving toward me, I have this." He pats his pistol.

Lucifer nods. "Very well."

They both watch as he makes his exit, and then they look down at their own plates for a while.

"Well," Rex says, "since we only have an hour, I think it's time to get down to business."

CHAPTER TWENTY-THREE

"I had to make sure you wouldn't find Melissa on your own," Rex continues. "I purged the internet of her records, and believe me, that wasn't cheap. I'm just glad she never did the social media thing.

"And you're right. This is all about what you did to me on Thanksgiving Day back when I was ten years old."

"It was a long time ago," Mickey says. "Get over it."

"Does it surprise you that I haven't? Try looking at it through my eyes. My big brother, my idol, suddenly lunges across the table at me and tries to kill me. Your face filled my vision as you choked me. I could see every pore, every pimple, even some nose hair. Your teeth were clenched, and there was a bit of drool in the corners of your mouth."

Rex falls silent, and Mickey looks around the

turkey to see that his brother is staring into his food. He might be mistaken, but he thinks he sees Rex's eyes shining with tears.

"You made me shit myself. Did you know that?"

No, Mickey didn't. He doesn't say anything, though.

"You literally scared the shit out of me. Do you even know how scary you are?"

Déjà vu.

Rex dabs at his eyes with a cloth napkin and clears his throat. "Whenever you were around after that, I made myself scarce. I did a pretty good job until we went to the orphanage. You might remember we were bunked together for a while, but I was soon able to trade with another kid. I wish I hadn't."

Mickey looks at the clock. Forty-five minutes remain. The turkey and the whiskey smell good, so he partakes of both.

"Your time in the orphanage was peachy fuckin' keen. If someone gave you shit, you gave it right back, usually with your fists. Nobody wanted to fuck with you. They were all scared of you, and I couldn't blame them. Do you know what happened to me?"

Mickey chews, waiting.

"The kid that I bunked with. He was one of the older kids. A bunch of them raped me. They passed me around like a sex doll. They tore me up. I felt so bad I can still feel them inside of me. I went to you for help, remember?"

Mickey remembers a time when Rex begged him for help. He never knew why, but he recalls how wretched Rex looked. He looked pathetic, and that disgusted Mickey.

"You remember," Rex says. "I see it on your face. Do you remember what you told me?"

He doesn't. It's a faded memory, and it never meant much to him.

"You told me to toughen up, and you called me a pussy."

That sounds like something Mickey would have said. It brings back no memory, but it makes sense.

"I was scared," Rex says. "I needed my big brother to stand up for me, and you cast me off like a cellophane wrapper. But even worse it reminded me of something Dad once said to me. When I was in second grade a bully punched me in the face and pushed me down. I cried to Dad about it, and can you guess what he had to say?"

Mickey looks at his gun which Lucifer had left by the turkey. It's a far way down the table, and he doubts he can get to it before Rex can shoot him.

There is a loud crash, and Mickey tenses up. Adrenaline squirts into his system, and he whips his head around, looking for whatever might be coming at him.

All he sees is Rex. His brother has stood up and has thrown his dishes to the floor. "You won't make it that far, Mickey. I just want you to look at me when I'm fucking talking to you."

Mickey settles back and takes a drink. His pulse slows a bit, and the flush in his face cools off.

Rex sits down. He spears a cheese square with a toothpick and sticks it into his mouth. When he finishes chewing he takes a sip of wine. "Dad told me that maybe if I wasn't such a faggot, I wouldn't have this bully problem. Can you believe that?"

Mickey nods. "He said the same thing to me."

Rex laughs, but it sounds like the mirth of a robotic clown. His mouth stretches out wide enough to jab a fist in, but his eyes are dead. "What next, brother? Are you going to tell me that he was just trying to turn me into a man?"

Mickey shrugs. "Who cares? Dad's dead. You need to stop blaming everyone else for your problems. Stand up on your own two feet. You should let it all go."

"Like you did?"

Mickey waits.

"You mean to tell me Dad doesn't bother you anymore? You mean to tell me that you're the way you are because you're so burden free?"

Mickey feels his lips pull back from his teeth, and something swims toward his throat. "You met the beast once. It's not baggage. It's an impulse. A very powerful impulse. Something you wouldn't understand."

"But Dad did, is that it?"

Mickey belts down the rest of his drink, and the beast retreats. He pours again. "Dad put it inside of me, and he knew it. It's going to be there until I die."

Rex smiles and looks up and behind him. "Which will be in about thirty-five minutes."

Mickey almost laughs. His brother might be right. He might be wrong, though. "Maybe you have a beast of your own, after all. How many people are dead because of you?"

"I lost count."

"Ever wonder why you do it?"

"No. I do it to get richer and to protect my money. Those are fairly legitimate reasons, no?"

"No. I think it makes you evil."

Rex pauses. "I don't know. Maybe. But at least I give back. I balance my life. For every person who has ever died because of me, I've given a shit load of money to some charity or other. Speaking of which, I don't ever recall you doing that. Child support is not the same thing. You sat in that apartment I gave you for how long? A couple of months? You never lacked for money and supplies. What did you spend your weekly two thousand on? Whiskey. Tools. More booze. When did you ever give back to some charity? You could have. How much do you have saved up because of me?"

"Doesn't matter. You can't balance your books by throwing a bone to some needy people. Maybe if your worst crime was jaywalking, but guess what?"

Mickey doesn't need to finish. Rex coughs hard when he hears this last part, and he gags and throws an entire glass of wine down his throat before he can stop.

"Fuck this. You have a half an hour to go. Eat up."

They eat in silence, not even bothering to make eye contact. Mickey thinks the food is very well prepared. It's the first good meal he's had since the night before Karnaki arrested him.

But it's so plentiful he is already feeling bloated. He checks the clock and sees he's down to twenty-five minutes.

Rex stops eating for a moment and examines

his brother. Mickey feels it, but he doesn't look up. He knows Rex will eventually continue pontificating. He's put too much effort into making this dinner happen.

"Do you think of yourself as the hero of this story?" Rex asks.

Mickey doesn't stop chewing in order to answer. "I'm an asshole just like everyone else."

Rex nibbles at the corner of his mouth and moves blocks of cheese around on his plate. He picks at it for a while, occasionally looking up at his brother.

Mickey glances up and lets out a tremendous sigh. He puts his utensils down and leans back in his chair. "Just say it."

"Hm?"

"Whatever's on your mind. You want to say it, so just say it."

Rex shakes his head. "It doesn't matter anymore. The plan didn't work. I'm glad I was able to fuck with you a bit, but . . ." He throws his hands up in a showy shrug.

"What else are we going to talk about?" Mickey asks. "Sports? The weather?"

Rex mulls this one over, bobbing his head back and forth. "Why not? I'm sure you followed my career. And now you know that I followed yours."

"No, I didn't keep tabs on you. I didn't even know who you were."

Rex's eyebrows furrow, and he picks a little too hard at his cheese. The perfect square comes apart in slivers. "Regardless. I knew you were crooked. I knew what you were doing to the streets of our beloved city. I had some of your partners on my payroll, and they told me everything about you."

Mickey tries to think back over his long line of partners and tries to determine who Rex is talking about. He quickly gives up; it doesn't matter all that much.

"I know you killed Sgt. Parker. For a fact."

"No, I didn't."

"When you die, you learn everything," Rex says. "But even if that didn't happen, you left plenty of evidence behind. The courts never got it, though. Ever wonder why?"

"You paid everyone off," Mickey says.

"Well. Yes. Obviously. But the thing is, I wanted revenge. I had ever since you turned your back on me. But now, as an adult, I suddenly had the means to make it happen. I couldn't get it if you were behind bars."

Rex pauses for a drink, and the wine seems to be having an effect on him. His eyes are filming over, and his hands aren't quite as steady as they used to be.

"I wanted you off balance. I wanted you doubting yourself. I wanted to take everything away from you. And I wanted to destroy you. But I wanted to be the agent that set all of it in motion, so I sent you to prison. I didn't want you to go down for something as dangerous as murder, so I made sure that charge disappeared."

"You're too kind."

Rex ignores him. "I hoped that prison would make you into an even bigger scumbag. Someone more open to suggestion. I hoped it would make you desperate."

Mickey pretends to drink from his glass. It's six-fifty.

"It was me who talked Melissa into divorcing

you. She had a new man in her life, so I figured I didn't have to work too hard to tear the two of you apart. I also convinced her not to ever bring your daughter to visit you. I was the middleman for all money exchanges. In short, you've never met Raquel because of me."

Mickey feels himself sinking into his body. The beast clogs his throat, and stars twinkle in his vision. *Not yet. Just wait a few more minutes.* He looks down to see a butter knife he's been holding is now bent savagely at the midpoint. *Just a few more minutes.*

"I got impatient, though. Maybe that was my mistake. I kept listening for stories about you, but you were too smart. You did many naughty things in there, and you got busted for none of them. I hear you cleaned that fucking place up. Did you really cut some poor bastard's face off?"

"Jake Peterson," Mickey says. "I did it with a razorblade stuck in a melted toothbrush. He shouldn't have tried to shank me."

Rex waves an impatient hand. "Right. But I wanted to really fuck you up. I wanted to destroy you. It was taking too much time, so I started paying people off to get you out early. I sent Lucifer Robinson and Lotho Chakur to pick you up because they're the creepiest motherfuckers I know, and they're very dangerous. I knew they'd turn your head into a spinning, chaotic mush, and Lucifer was clever enough to keep it that way. Would you care to know what their jobs were?"

Mickey doesn't dare open his mouth. He's afraid the beast will come out, and he needs to keep it together a little while longer. *Just seven more minutes.*

"I heard about how killing Parker really messed with your mind. It made you fear yourself. And no matter how badly you fucked people up, you never killed them. That was your line, and I wanted to make you cross it. Lucifer was supposed to work you up to it. Slowly. Give you a few delivery jobs, then work you up to breaking kneecaps and so on. And then he was supposed to seduce you into becoming a killer, one of the few things you've always despised. Do you remember when we were kids, and you always talked about becoming a cop?"

Mickey nods.

"Do you remember what you told me?"

Mickey nods again.

"Say it."

"I wanted to make the killers pay." Mickey speaks through his clenched teeth, and he can feel the beast trying to squirm out through the small gaps between them.

"That was your line, and you swore you'd never cross it. And then you killed Parker. Then you started wondering what you were turning into."

Mickey feels his fingernails digging into his palms, and his entire body trembles, trying desperately to hold the beast in. Darkness inches into the corners of his vision.

"I wanted you to cross that line again and again and again, and I wanted it to tear whatever passes for your soul to pieces. I wanted you to agonize over it until you just couldn't take it anymore. And then, just when you've finally broken to pieces, I was going to be there to laugh in your face. As soon as you recognized me, I was going to strangle you to death. I would have probably needed Lotho's help, but I would have done it."

Rex pauses long enough to take another sip of wine. "But I guess it just wasn't meant to be. You were too smart. I still don't know how you figured it out, but I think it might have been Uncle Jack. Was it?"

Mickey can't answer him even if he wanted to. His body is petrified in his attempt to keep the beast in. He tries envisioning himself chopping a tree down with his bare hands, but nothing lessens the feeling in his guts.

Rex turns to look at the clock. "In five minutes I'm going to kill you. And then I'm going to go out and see Melissa at your old place. I'm going to give her the tragic news about your death, and I'm going to fuck her silly. Because I'm a sensitive guy, and because it's not the first time we've done it." He laughs and picks up the semi-auto. "Mickey, I have to tell you, and I cannot express my sheer joy in this moment, but paternity tests are no good if the fathers in question are brothers. Raquel is *my* daughter."

Mickey roars, and the beast explodes out of his mouth. In less than a second he is covered in coarse fur, and his teeth are fangs. It feels like a film of slime coating his skin as it completely encapsulates him, sending him deep into his own mind. A look of uncertainty comes across Rex's face, and the gun wavers in his hand. But as soon as he sees the thing that had been Mickey Scarlet kick his chair back, Rex takes aim and fires.

He's had too much wine. The bullet sails far astray.

Mickey is a homunculus inside his brain,

peering out at the world through the windows of his eyes. He is barely aware of it as he braces his feet against the floor and lets out a werewolf's howl. His hands go to the table, and with a tremendous, adrenaline-fueled push, the large wooden slab scrapes across the marble floor. It surges forward and catches Rex in the chest, shoving him back against the clock. The semi-auto barks again, and once more the bullet misses and plows into the ceiling.

The grandfather clock bongs and explodes into splinters. Gears roll over the floor, and the pendulum, like a lizard's molted tail, slaps the marble just under Rex's chair. Three numbers fall and get stuck in Rex's hair: seven, five and what might be either a six or a nine.

Mickey pushes himself up and strides toward his brother. Somewhere deep inside his mind he recognizes the junkie's gun on the table, and he wants to pick it up. The beast won't let him. It's too single-minded, and there is nothing on earth that can stop it.

Rex shakes the numbers from his hair and looks up in time to see Mickey advancing on him. Gritting his teeth, he pulls the gun back up, but he's still drunk, and the sudden violence has unfocused his eyes. They roll in their sockets like balls. He blinks, but by then it's too late. Mickey twists the gun from Rex's hand, snapping his trigger finger, and throws it across the room. The gun explodes and shatters to pieces.

Mickey wraps his hands around his brother's throat, and it feels like they'd been born there. He squeezes. Rex's good fingers try to slip under the thick pads of Mickey's palms, but they're just not strong enough. As his face turns red, then purple, and his eyes begin to bulge, his fingernails scrabble at his brother's muscular arms, unable to find purchase.

Hands pull at Mickey's shoulders, and an arm wraps around his neck, trying to pull him away from his brother. He snarls, whipping his head around to see his father. Blood no longer dribbles from the wound on his forehead; it gushes.

Maxwell pauses, and he draws away. "Never mind, kid. It's got you."

He fades into nothingness, and the cloud of what he was disperses.

The beast turns back to Rex. Homunculus Mickey watches his brother suffocate, and he feels nothing. There is a curious fascination in having lost control, in witnessing things he's doing, things he can't stop himself from doing.

His fingers strain, and he can see the blood vessels standing out under the hirsute skin on his arms. He can see his hands sinking into Rex's darkening flesh. His knuckles look like chips of rock, and his thumbnails are pale ghosts floating just under his brother's chin.

Rex's pretty blue eyes roll up, and his slender cheeks bloat out. Still his hands flutter at Mickey's as his tongue pokes out of his purple lips. Saliva glistens in the corners of his mouth, and a faint gurgling sound comes from deep in his throat.

Finally Rex's hands fall away, and the gurgling peters out. Mickey keeps the pressure on and squeezes until his hands creak. Rex's flesh turns gray and flakes away. Something hot bakes through his body, and red glows in the cracks of his skin. His eyes drop into his skull, and flames shoot out of the empty sockets. A corona of fire circles his head like a hellish halo.

Rex's skin is gone, and Mickey tightly grasps a bare spinal column. The bones crack under his strength, and the fiery corpse explodes. Shards of him fly out around the room leaving smoky trails. All that remains of him are tiny bone splinters sticking into Mickey's hands.

Slowly he feels himself fading back in. He's no longer a witness to his actions, and he can feel the ragged breath tearing through his lungs. He can hear the grinding sound of his clenched teeth. A slight burning sensation touches his palms, and he sees they're covered in ashes. He blows them away and even the small bits of Rex collapse and drift away.

Something clicks in the destroyed grandfather clock, and it makes seven clinks. Seven o'clock.

Mickey stands and straightens out. He heads back to the table and picks up the junkie's gun. The beast is satisfied, but he knows he'll need to fight his way out of here. Lucifer, Lotho, the guards and, of course, the hell dogs.

But first . . . he heads back to his end of the table and pours a tall drink. He gulps it down and feels it slow-burn through his body. A flush runs up his sore arms. His shoulders slump, and he relaxes just a little bit.

Mickey takes up Raggedy Ann and looks into her button eyes. She looks as happy as ever, and he can't wait to see the look on Raquel's face when he gives her the doll. For now he stuffs it in his pocket and turns to leave.

Lotho stands in the doorway, his eyes covered

with his ubiquitous sunglasses. The chauffeur's cap is gone, and in the flickering light from the burning chandelier, Mickey can see shadows dancing in the soup bowl dents in Lotho's skull.

He holds a pale object between both of his large, scarred hands. They turn it around and around like he's a pitcher seeking a grip on a baseball. After a moment, Mickey realizes what it is.

Willie Salas's head.

"Twisted it off like I was taking the lid off a jar," Lotho says. He smiles, showing off his sharp, cannibal teeth.

Mickey lifts the gun and aims it at Lotho's chest.

"You can't kill me," Lotho says. "No one can."

Mickey fires, and a red flower blooms behind Lotho's tie. The old man's head tumbles from his grip and rolls across the floor. It stops at Mickey's feet, and its flat, colorless eyes gaze up at him.

Lotho touches his wound and lets the blood soak his shirt. If he feels pain, he doesn't show it. Instead he starts walking slowly toward Mickey, grinning.

Mickey fires again, aiming for Lotho's mouth, but he misses. The shot disintegrates his nose instead. The giant remains silent as he stalks forward.

This time Mickey aims for Lotho's forehead, and a new hole appears at the top of his bald dome. The exit wound tears out a large part of the back of his head. Blood and chunks of brain ooze out like yolk from a broken egg, and Mickey swears this has to do the job.

It doesn't stop Lotho. Now he's three yards

away, and he charges, howling a war cry so loud and shrill it almost makes Mickey shit himself. He tries to get off another shot, but he's not fast enough. Lotho takes him low in the belly, and they both tumble across the table, sending food and plates and utensils crashing about the marble floor as if someone has dropped a drum kit down a set of stairs.

Lotho's gore-streaked sausage fingers seek Mickey's throat, and he tries to back-slither out from under the giant's body. It's too late. Powerful hands encircle his throat and lock down, instantly pinching out his breath. Stars dance before his eyes.

Mickey knows he's fucked. While he still has the strength, he throws a few punches into Lotho's small ribs at his armpits. They bounce off as if the giant's skin is made of rubber. Mickey tries to get his hands between their bodies in hopes of jabbing a finger into the driver's chest wound, but they're too close together.

Darkness fills the corners of Mickey's eyes, and he wonders where the beast is when he needs it most. Is it taking a nap in the back of his mind?

He considers the ragged hole where Lotho's nose had been, and he wonders if he can cause the giant pain by sticking his fingers in there. Probably not.

That leaves one thing.

Mickey's hands crawl up the driver's face like spiders, and when he's close enough, he shoves his fingers into Lotho's eyes. Mickey's left arm isn't strong enough, and it gives up and drops to the floor. His right arm still has some juice, and he feels his thumb sink in. Lotho's eye pops like a ripe berry, and fluid drips down his cheek.

But Lotho does not scream. He does not recoil. He does not falter.

He squeezes harder.

Mickey's tongue oozes between his teeth and parts his lips. The darkness encroaches upon the rest of his vision, and he knows he'll never get to meet his daughter. His right hand falls away from Lotho's ruined face, leaving a slug-trail of vitreous fluid and blood. It falls into a pile of broken china and utensils.

He feels a steak knife against his palm.

I have to see Raquel.

Mickey twists his hand so he can grip the knife's blade. He squeezes it as hard as he can. The thought of dropping it scares him more than anything has ever scared him before.

With all the force he can muster, he slices the tendons in Lotho's left arm. Instantly the fingers on one side of his throat are limp, and he quickly darts for the giant's other arm.

Lotho roars—not in pain but with *rage*—and tries to block Mickey's attack. It's too late. The other hand comes loose, and air pours into Mickey's lungs. The darkness is gone, and his face tingles as blood returns to where it belongs.

Lotho tries to grab his wounds, but his fingers don't work. His remaining eye glares down at Mickey, and he draws his skull back for a head butt.

Mickey doesn't waste time. He stabs the blade into Lotho's throat, pinning his Adam's apple to his spine. Finally, something gives in Lotho's sturdy foundation, and he tumbles backward, freeing Mickey completely.

Lotho grabs for him, but Mickey slips away, surprised that the giant has anything left in him. The steak knife pokes out of his throat like a candle on a birthday cake, and his face is a bloody ruin. His fingers dangle uselessly from the ends of his hands.

Yet he's still ready to fight.

"Just fucking die already," Mickey says. His voice is gravelly and hoarse.

Lotho tries to stand. There is no pain on his face, only anger. His teeth scrape against each other, and he looks like he very much has the ability to continue fighting.

Mickey grabs a plate and throws it at the giant's face. It shatters, and the pieces fall like hailstones at his feet. Lotho doesn't falter. He can't get himself all the way up, but he's crawling toward Mickey.

Mickey finds another steak knife and holds it up, flashing it at Lotho's remaining eye. He hopes this will be enough to convince the giant to give up, but he knows better.

Fuck it. Instead of waiting, Mickey lunges forward, putting another blade into Lotho's throat. This time he holds onto it and jerks it out. He stabs Lotho again and again and again.

Lotho gags, blood running down his face from the corner of his mouth. His movements become less coordinated, and Mickey knows he's finally making progress. He stabs Lotho's throat until it's a pulpy mess, and then he moves on to Lotho's face.

The driver finally drops down all the way to the floor, but Mickey wants to make sure. He sits on the giant's chest and continues stabbing Lotho's face. He puts out the remaining eye and jabs the blade into the bullet hole, stirring Lotho's brains around like he's getting ready to bake a cake.

The blood stops pumping and merely runs out of Lotho. When Mickey sees this, he decides he's done. Lotho is unquestionably dead. He leaves the knife in Lotho's giant head and stands, reaching for the whiskey once more. He can barely breathe, and he sees that he's covered in blood. He can't meet his daughter like *this*.

He checks in his pocket for Raggedy Ann, and she's still clean. At least he has this much going for him.

Mickey goes to pick up his gun, but it's no longer where he'd left it. He hears a click and looks up to see Lucifer Robinson standing over Lotho's body. He holds Mickey's gun.

"Tsk," Lucifer says. "I really wish you hadn't killed Lotho."

CHAPTER TWENTY-FOUR

Mickey picks up the whiskey bottle and pours himself another drink. He wonders if he can throw the bottle at Lucifer, to throw him off balance, so he can rush him and get the gun back. It's not a good idea, but it's *an* idea.

Lucifer chuckles and cracks open the cylinder. He dumps the bullets out to the floor and kicks them away before closing the gun and leaving it on the table. "I think we've had enough killing for one day, don't you?"

"That depends," Mickey says. "Are you going to stop me from getting out of here?"

"Why should I? My boss is dead, so I'm no longer on retainer."

Mickey starts toward the door, but Lucifer steps in his path. "There's one thing you should consider before you walk out those doors."

"I've got nothing to say to you." Mickey tries to walk around Lucifer, but again he blocks the exit.

"You don't get it. This isn't Rex Paolo's house anymore. It's yours, and everything that comes with it. Mr. Scarlet, you're a billionaire. All you have to do is fill your brother's shoes."

"Not interested."

This time Lucifer lets him pass. Just as Mickey gets to the door, the pallid gentleman turns toward him. "You'd rather see your family than be rich beyond your wildest imagination? The fact is, your ex-wife doesn't love you, and your daughter doesn't know you. But I have more women at my beck and call than you could possibly imagine. Do you want a different woman for every day of the week? I can do that. You can marry them all and start a family of families. Families that *will* love you. When was the last time you heard someone say that they love you?"

Mickey feels something tug at the back of his collar, and for a brief pants-shitting moment he thinks Lotho isn't dead after all. He whirls around, but there is no one there. Then he feels something crawling like a bug on his shoulder. He looks down and sees a small demon. And another. And another. They're women, and they all have horned heads and pointed tails. Their breasts are too big for their frail bodies. All of them tug at him, whispering in his ear. *You can have anything you want. Who wouldn't want that?*

Lucifer approaches. "Anything your heart desires. Love is a commodity, and it's a cheap one. You can have as much of it as you want. All you have to do is be your brother. How hard is that?"

"You mean, be a mobster?" Mickey asks.

"There are no mobsters anymore," Lucifer says. "Just businessmen." He holds out the junkie's gun and a handful of bullets, each in separate hands. Mickey takes them, barely being aware of it.

Instead he thinks of Raquel. Is she worth a kingdom?

Yes. That and more. "Fuck you. I don't want any family. I want *mine*. Hell, I just want my daughter."

Lucifer sighs and looks down at his feet. Very quietly he steps back and gestures to the door. Mickey grabs the doorknob and starts to turn it.

"Don't go. Stay here. Be powerful. You can't imagine the kinds of fun we can have. The power is intoxicating. You could live like a king."

Mickey pauses. "It worked out pretty well for Rex, didn't it?" He opens the door.

"Out there lies nothing but doom," Lucifer says. "You won't be under our protection anymore. Do you believe you can just walk away from this?"

"You know where to find me," Mickey says. He holds up the empty gun. "I love dogs. I'd never dream of hurting them. But if it comes down to me or them, I'll shoot them. Do I have to shoot them?"

"No. The hellhounds won't bother you."

"Good."

"Give my regards to Sgt. Parker," Lucifer says. "I get the feeling you're going to see him very soon."

Mickey grunts and goes through the door, leaving Lucifer in a room of the dead. He goes through the corridor until he finds the double doors at the front. Two guards wait, and for a moment Mickey thinks they'll be trouble. Then they merely open the doors for him, and he steps out into the dusk. He stalks down the long drive, and in the corners of his eyes, he sees dark shapes darting about the lawn. Some of them pause long enough to watch his passage, but none of them try to stop him.

The gate opens before him, and he sees the impaled damned screaming and writhing. He walks past them, trying to not make eye contact. As soon as he's out on the street, the world goes silent. He turns and sees an ordinary set of gates, broken and rusty. Through the opening in the wall, Mickey sees nothing but an empty field. The foundation of what might have been a grand house marks the ground, and just beyond it stands Lucifer Robinson, leaning on his cane and grinning at Mickey.

Mickey turns away. There are no cars out here, so he figures he'll have to walk to his old house. It's only two, maybe three miles, and he can hike that, no problem. He takes out his cell phone, planning on calling Melissa to let her know that he's running late, and to please not leave before he arrives. Then he remembers that he doesn't have her number.

He calls Uncle Jack, but all he gets is voicemail. He leaves a message and drops his phone in his pocket along with Raggedy Ann. He loads the junkie's gun, even though he probably won't need it. This thing is over. There shouldn't be any further danger. Still, it's better to be prepared.

"Mickey Scarlet!"

He pauses. The voice is feminine, and it sounds

very familiar. There is anger in it, and Mickey wonders if maybe Melissa came looking for him.

He turns, but it isn't his ex-wife. It's Inez Parker, and she's aiming a gun at him.

Mickey opens his mouth to say something, but her gun speaks first. He feels his guts turn to mush. She fires again and again, taking deliberate aim at his belly and tearing it to shreds. Mickey feels his legs go weak, and they're going to fold under him. He knows it. He tries to keep on his feet.

Inez raises the pistol, aiming at his face, and Mickey's gun hand flies up on instinct. He fires everything he's got in her direction. He never thinks about it. It just happens.

She doesn't even yelp as her brains jump out the back of her head. She can't because one of the other slugs has torn out her throat. The final bullets take her in the chest, driving her to the ground in a pile.

Now Mickey falls, and his guts try to escape through his Swiss cheesed stomach. It feels like a gallon of blood is pressing his pants to his legs, and he holds his hand to the holes in his belly. Blood soaks his fingers and spills over them.

He looks over to Inez's body and wonders where the fuck she came from. Is this another of Lucifer's games? The gun. It looks familiar. Then he remembers that Karnaki had one just like it strapped to his ankle on the day he'd arrested Mickey. Is it possible—?

Mickey doesn't care anymore. He just wants to lie down and let whatever remains of his life ebb away.

He almost does this, but his hand grazes

Raggedy Ann in his pocket. If he doesn't meet Raquel now, he never will.

Mickey shrugs out of his jacket and whips it around until it's one thick line of cloth. He presses it against his ruined belly and ties it on tightly. He grimaces, expecting a world of pain, but he feels nothing. He thinks he's in shock. Weakness slows him down, but now that he has a sense of purpose, nothing will stop him.

He staggers toward Inez's body. A mere few minutes ago he would have felt sorry for her. She certainly didn't deserve any of this. But he just doesn't care now.

He takes her purse from around her dead arm and goes through it until he finds her car keys. He hits the button on the fob, and about a half-mile away, he sees a car flashing its lights. He stumbles toward it, his feet seemingly encased in cement blocks, but he gets to it and gets in. He sets Raggedy Ann on the passenger seat and turns the key in the ignition.

CHAPTER TWENTY-FIVE

The jacket isn't enough to keep the blood at bay. The cloth is saturated quickly, and soon he feels fresh warm blood pour into his lap again. Grimacing, he presses his free hand against the wound. It doesn't do much good, but it helps keep his guts in.

Blood loss is making him a bit lightheaded, but he's able to keep his senses about him. He'd driven drunk many times, and this is kind of like that. His head tilts to one side, and the road goes off at all angles. He knows where he is going, though. The car handles a little differently than the one he's used to, but he keeps it on the road and going at a pretty decent clip. Well over the speed limit.

Mickey glances up into the rearview mirror, and he thinks he sees someone in the back seat. He adjusts the mirror and looks again, but he sees nothing.

239

Please don't let me die. Not yet. I'm almost there.

He takes a curve at ninety miles per hour. The tires squeal, begging to slip from the road. Traction remains, and he straightens out before the car can go into a skid.

Sweat jumps off his brow and lands on his cheek just below his eye. He moves his belly hand to wipe it away, but when he does, something inside of him shifts. He puts his hand back, which is for the best. All the gore on it would have made matters worse.

In the dark he rockets past the stump of a tree. The ghost of what once had been there watches as he passes and mourns at the short memory of mankind.

A finger accidentally slips into one of the holes in his belly and brushes a piece of intestine. He gags and pulls it out. There is no pain from the contact, but it feels very unpleasant. He tries to unravel the jacket a little so it covers more space.

He holds on tightly as he feels himself slipping away. The road disappears under the hood of his car, and he knows it just isn't fast enough. He pushes it to a hundred and watches the pavement rush by.

There! Silhouetted against the final dying rays of the sun, a black shape against the cobalt sky. He sees his old house and the gravel road which leads to it. He whips the wheel around and goes off the road. He skids across the grass and leaves gaping wounds in the ground, but he turns the wheel again and puts himself back on course.

One eye closes, and the other descends halfway. For a moment everything goes dim, and a bony hand from the backseat gently touches his shoulder. Mickey bites his lower lip hard enough for his teeth to meet through his flesh, and the hand goes away. He's alone in the car again.

The house draws closer, and he can see one of the windows is lit up. The front room. Is she sitting in his old easy chair, or the couch? What is little Raquel doing? Playing with dolls? Talking with her mother?

Gravel grinds beneath his screaming tires, and he wonders if maybe he should have taken Lucifer's deal. No, he'd made the right decision. If he'd stuck with Lucifer Robinson, he knows he'd have whatever he wanted in the world, but it would be empty.

He blinks the sweat from his eyes and rubs his wet face against the sleeve of his jacket. He keeps his hand over his wounds, and nothing slips out from the holes.

Mickey's foot falls from the accelerator, and he presses the brake down. The car slows, and he parks in his old driveway. There are cracks and weeds sprouting out that he doesn't remember, not even from his last visit to this place.

It's okay. I'll fix it after Melissa takes me back.

He picks up Raggedy Ann while his other hand fumbles around in the dark for the handle. In his car it's in his armrest, but here it is near the side mirror adjuster. It takes him a second before he can pop the door open. He slides out as if he's seated in grease, and he barely notices that the cushion is now a blood sponge.

Mickey takes two steps before his feet fold together, dropping him face first into the dirt. This time his hand isn't enough to keep his guts in. A short loop slips out, and he gingerly stuffs it back in with a mud smeared finger.

Resting on his knees, he unravels the jacket a bit more and turns it to the side least soaked in blood. Again he presses it to his belly with one besmirched hand while holding the doll in the other, shuffling his way up to the porch.

His feet clamp on the wooden steps, and the structure creaks as if it's on its last legs. His shoes scrape as he makes his way to the front door. The screen is easy enough to push aside. It screeches on its hinges and then falls away, clattering to the porch.

Hafta fixit later.

Mickey holds Raggedy Ann between his index finger and thumb while the rest of his left hand works at the knob. He can barely feel the metal against his palm as it rattles and jangles. It takes a couple of turns before he can push through the door.

There is Melissa, standing by the fireplace, jabbing at the smoldering wood with a long metal rod. When she hears the door open she looks up, a slight smile on her face. She looks good. Perfect shape. Her slender face glows from a wreath of gorgeous curly hair. Time has done well with her, and he wants nothing more than to hold her in his arms and kiss her for the rest of eternity.

Mickey doesn't register the middle-aged man off to his right, reading something on his phone. Mickey's eyes go straight to the little girl sitting on the couch, her nose buried in a book. It's a yellow Nancy Drew volume, and she is three-quarters of the way through. So reading is no chore for her, and Mickey feels proud.

But there is none of him in this girl's face. Mickey decides it's for the best, considering how ugly he is. Raquel bears the same good looks that had worked in Rex's favor. A thick head of dark hair, full lips, a slender nose. Soft features, something that might land her a modeling job someday. Something that will definitely get her in trouble with boys.

From the corner of his eye he sees Melissa's features change. She must have seen the blood. The poker falls from her hand, and her face turns oblong. She touches her mouth with her bird-like hands.

Mickey holds the doll out to Raquel before he realizes that the stuffing has been knocked out of it by one of Inez Parker's bullets. There's a powder burn in Raggedy Ann's tummy, and her face is covered in Mickey's bloody fingerprints.

"I brought you something, darling," he says. Except it doesn't come out that way. All he hears is a garbled, mush-mouthed mess, and it takes him a moment to realize the sound came from himself.

Raquel looks up from her book, and the instant she sees Mickey she screams. The book drops from her lap and thwacks shut on the floor. His ears ring with the sound of the little girl's fear, and Melissa's own shrill cry joins it.

"What?" he tries to ask. But he understands. He doesn't need a mirror to know what he must look like.

He tries to step forward, but he slumps to his knees instead. Still he pushes the doll forward like some kind of peace offering. Blood glistens in Raggedy Ann's eyes, and Raquel pushes herself back further into the couch.

"Don't be afraid," Mickey says. "I love you."

Melissa scoops up the fireplace poker and points it at him. "You stay the fuck away from my daughter!"

"Holy Christ!" the man says. He's frozen in place in his chair.

Mickey falls forward, cracking his head on the floor. His skin goes numb at the point of impact. The doll flies from his hand, and he examines the grain in the wooden planks before his eyes.

Melissa lunges at him, slamming the poker into his back, but he barely feels it. Maybe once upon a time the beast would have slithered out of him and given him a last boost of energy. Not now. It's gone. The beast is dead, and its corpse is probably resting next to Inez Parker's body.

Mickey inches forward and reaches his hand toward his daughter's foot, which barely hangs off the edge of the couch. She's wearing sandals, and her pale flesh shines out to him. Something falls out of him and slaps wetly against the floor, but it doesn't matter to him. He just needs to make contact.

The tips of his fingers brush against the side of Raquel's foot. A static charge runs through his body, and he can feel her warmth and the beating of her heart.

"I'm sorry," he whispers. "I . . ."

Mickey falls away, and he keeps on falling.

Forever.

THE END

ABOUT THE AUTHOR

John Bruni is the author of several books, most recently AND JESUS CAME BACK from Rooster Republic Press. His short fiction has appeared in a variety of publications, such as A HACKED-UP HOLIDAY MASSACRE (from Pill Hill Press, edited by Shane McKenzie) and SHROUD MAGAZINE. He edited STRANGE SEX 3 for StrangeHouse Books. He lives in Elmhurst, IL, where he promises he's not as violent as you would think. He's only ever punched two people over the course of forty years.